Cause & Effect: The American Revolution

Hal Marcovitz

San Diego, CA

973.3 Marcovitz
Marcovitz, Hal.
The American Revolution

About the Author

Hal Marcovitz is a former newspaper reporter and columnist and the author of more than 170 books for young readers. He grew up in Philadelphia and now makes his home in Bucks County, Pennsylvania. In 1776 George Washington launched his Christmas night attack on the Hessians from Taylorsville, a town in Bucks County.

© 2016 ReferencePoint Press, Inc.
Printed in the United States

For more information, contact:
ReferencePoint Press, Inc.
PO Box 27779
San Diego, CA 92198
www.ReferencePointPress.com

ALL RIGHTS RESERVED.
No part of this work covered by the copyright hereon may be reproduced or used in any form or by any means—graphic, electronic, or mechanical, including photocopying, recording, taping, web distribution, or information storage retrieval systems—without the written permission of the publisher.

LIBRARY OF CONGRESS CATALOGING-IN-PUBLICATION DATA

Marcovitz, Hal.
  Cause & effect: the American Revolution / by Hal Marcovitz.
      pages cm. -- (Cause & effect in history)
  Includes bibliographical references and index.
  Audience: Grade 9 to 12.
  ISBN-13: 978-1-60152-790-5 (hardback)
  ISBN-10: 1-60152-790-X (hardback)
  1. United States--History--Revolution, 1775-1783--Juvenile literature. I. Title. II. Title: American Revolution.
  E208.M3394 2015
  973.3--dc23
                                                                                2015000432

CONTENTS

Foreword	4
Important Events in the American Revolution	6
Introduction Assault on Breed's Hill	8
Chapter One A Brief History of the American Revolution	12
Chapter Two How Did the Actions by the King and Parliament Give Rise to the Revolution?	24
Chapter Three How Did the Battles of Trenton and Princeton Change the Course of the Revolution?	36
Chapter Four How Did Assistance from France Help the American Cause?	48
Chapter Five How Did the American Revolution Spark Change Throughout the World?	60
Source Notes	72
For Further Research	75
Index	77
Picture Credits	80

FOREWORD

"History is a complex study of the many causes that have influenced happenings of the past and the complicated effects of those varied causes."

—William & Mary School of Education,
Center for Gifted Education

Understanding the causes and effects of historical events is rarely simple. The fall of Rome, for instance, had many causes. The onslaught of barbarians from the north, the weakening of Rome's economic and military foundations, and internal disunity are often cited as contributing to Rome's collapse. Yet even when historians generally agree on a primary cause (in this instance, the barbarian invasions) leading to a specific outcome (that is, Rome's fall), they also agree that other conditions at the time influenced the course of those events. Under different conditions, the effect might have been something else altogether.

The value of analyzing cause and effect in history, therefore, is not necessarily to identify a single cause for a singular event. The real value lies in gaining a greater understanding of history as a whole and being able to recognize the many factors that give shape and direction to historic events. As outlined by the National Center for History in the Schools at the University of California–Los Angeles, these factors include "the importance of the individual in history ... the influence of ideas, human interests, and beliefs; and ... the role of chance, the accidental and the irrational."

ReferencePoint's Cause & Effect in History series examines major historic events by focusing on specific causes and consequences. For instance, in *Cause & Effect: The French Revolution*, a chapter explores how inequality led to the revolution. And in *Cause & Effect: The American Revolution*, one chapter delves into this question: "How did assistance from France help the American cause?" Every book in the series includes thoughtful discussion of questions like these—supported by facts, examples, and a mix of fully documented primary and secondary source quotes. Each title also includes an overview of the event so that readers have a broad context for understanding the more detailed discussions of specific causes and their effects.

The value of such study is not limited to the classroom; it can also be applied to many areas of contemporary life. The ability to analyze and interpret history's causes and consequences is a form of critical thinking. Critical thinking is crucial in many professions, ranging from law enforcement to science. Critical thinking is also essential for developing an educated citizenry that fully understands the rights and obligations of living in a free society. The ability to sift through and analyze complex processes and events and identify their possible outcomes enables people in that society to make important decisions.

The *Cause & Effect in History* series has two primary goals. One is to help students think more critically about history and develop a true understanding of its complexities. The other is to help build a foundation for those students to become fully participating members of the society in which they live.

IMPORTANT EVENTS IN THE AMERICAN REVOLUTION

1754
The French and Indian War erupts when the French attempt to control trade in the Ohio Valley; the war ends seven years later in a British victory.

1764
To pay off the British government's debts incurred during the French and Indian War, Parliament passes the Sugar Act, the first of several taxes imposed on the colonies.

1770
Five Bostonians are killed by British troops when a riot breaks out on March 5; eight soldiers are charged with murder in the Boston Massacre but are acquitted.

1774
Parliament passes the Intolerable Acts to curb rebellious behavior in Massachusetts; to frame a response to the harsh measures the Continental Congress begins meeting in Philadelphia.

1761 1764 1767 1770 1773

1763
King George III issues the Proclamation of 1763, prohibiting settlement in the colonies west of the Allegheny Mountains.

1772
Rhode Island colonists board the British warship *Gaspee*, force the crew ashore, then set the ship ablaze.

1765
Parliament passes the Quartering Act, requiring colonists to board British soldiers in their homes; civil disobedience over Parliament's taxes erupts in Boston, when a mob demolishes the Customs House.

1773
Colonists disguised as Indians stage the Boston Tea Party; they board merchant ships anchored in Boston Harbor and dump heavily taxed British tea overboard.

1775
Rebellious colonists defeat the Redcoats at Lexington and Concord on April 19 but lose the Battle of Breed's Hill on June 17, although the British sustain heavy casualties in the skirmish.

1781
The British army under Charles Cornwallis surrenders after the Battle of Yorktown in Virginia, ending the Revolution.

1777
The British army's defeat at Saratoga, New York, helps convince Louis XVI, king of France, to aid the Revolution. Washington's army spends a cold winter at Valley Forge in Pennsylvania.

1783
The Treaty of Paris is signed on September 3; Great Britain recognizes the independence of its former colonies in America.

1787
Delegates from the former American colonies draft a constitution that binds the individual states into a single, unified nation.

1776 1779 1782 1785 1788

1778
On February 6 France and the American colonies sign a treaty in which France recognizes the sovereignty of the United States of America and pledges military and financial aid to the Revolution.

1789
France's Estates-General issues the Declaration of the Rights of Man and Citizen, a document based on the principles of the Declaration of Independence.

1776
Congress adopts the Declaration of Independence. In August the British rout George Washington's army at the Battle of Brooklyn. In December Washington's troops regroup and win a decisive victory at the Battle of Trenton.

1792
After four years of war and insurrection French radicals abolish the monarchy. Louis XVI and the French queen, Marie-Antoinette, are executed the following year.

INTRODUCTION

Assault on Breed's Hill

The Battle of Breed's Hill—also known as the Battle of Bunker Hill—was waged on June 17, 1775, less than two months after the first battle of the American Revolution. In that battle colonial militiamen routed British troops at Lexington and Concord in Massachusetts. Shortly after Lexington and Concord, British general John Burgoyne described the victorious colonial militiamen with contempt when he called them, "A rabble in arms, flushed with success and insolence."[1]

Burgoyne's attitude reflected the view of the British military command as well as that of King George III and Lord Frederick North, the prime minister. They believed their army had been caught by surprise and, following the British retreat, vowed to take the offensive against the colonists. The American Revolution, the British believed, would be put down quickly once these untrained, ill-armed, and poorly led colonial militias encountered the true might of the British army.

Says historian John Ferling, "North's government agreed on one point: the Americans would pose little challenge in the event of war. The Americans had neither a standing army nor a navy; few among them were experienced officers. Britain possessed a professional army and the world's greatest navy."[2] But as events unfolded at Breed's Hill, North, Burgoyne, and others in the British government and military found their attitudes changing.

The Three Hills

To smash the Revolution the British recognized the strategic advantage of occupying the Charlestown peninsula south of Boston. The peninsula is a finger of land that extends into the Charles River, which virtually surrounds Boston. By occupying the peninsula, the British believed, they could control ship traffic in and out of Boston Harbor. Three hills dominate the peninsula. By occupying the hills—Bunker, Breed's, and Moulton's—the British knew they could fire down on merchant ships ferrying supplies into the rebellious colony and also provide cover for their own warships transporting troops and supplies into Boston. The British already had troops occupying Boston—they fled to the city after the rout at Lexington and Concord. To occupy the three hills, the British planned to send troops across the Charles River to take possession of the peninsula.

Word of the British plans leaked out. To keep the British from occupying the peninsula a regiment of about one thousand militiamen from Massachusetts and New Hampshire, under the command of Colonel William Prescott, assembled at the town of Cambridge, north of Boston. They marched quickly and quietly, entering the peninsula over land. They arrived the night of June 16, a day ahead of the British. Upon arriving on the peninsula Prescott ordered the men to dig trenches and build redoubts—tiny fortifications of earth, timber, and

An American lithograph showing the Battle of Bunker Hill. Both the British and colonials recognized the importance of occupying the heights that commanded the Charles River and the port of Boston.

rocks. These fortifications would provide cover against British fire. The colonists worked all night and were still working when dawn broke.

March up Breed's Hill

Camped nearby was the British attack force under General William Howe, who decided to attempt a landing along the southeastern shore of the peninsula. Due to low tide Howe could not make the landing until early afternoon. He crossed the river with fifteen hundred men aboard twenty-eight barges, landing at about 1 p.m. As the Redcoats approached the landing point, British ships anchored nearby opened fire on the peninsula, raining cannon fire down on the colonists.

Howe ordered the attack to begin. The British soldiers carried weapons as well as backpacks weighted down with ammunition, blankets, and rations. Side by side the Redcoats marched up the hill toward the colonists' position. This was a typical tactic of the era—armies usually faced one another as gentlemen, bravely facing fire and returning fire. "It was a blazing hot summer's day," says historian Benson Bobrick, "and the troops were absurdly encumbered with blankets, knapsacks, and provisions, altogether weighing 125 pounds per man. This was particularly fatiguing for those obliged to march up the hill's steep slope through the tall thick summer grass."[3]

Opening Volleys

The Americans held their fire. Prescott had given the order, "Don't one of you fire until you see the whites of their eyes."[4] Closer and closer marched the British. And then, when the Redcoats were no more than fifteen paces from the first line of trenches and redoubts, the colonists opened fire. Dozens of Redcoats fell dead in the opening volleys. The British gamely pressed on, trying to make it up the slope of Breed's Hill under heavy fire while carrying their overloaded backpacks. Many British soldiers were mowed down until, finally, Howe ordered a retreat.

Below the hill the British regrouped and tried a new assault. For more than two hours the Redcoats attempted to scale the hill, but again they were thrown back. As the survivors regrouped below the hill a second time, Howe surveyed his bloodied men. "[It was] a moment I never felt before,"[5] he said later.

Joined by reinforcements, Howe launched a third assault. Unknown to the British general, by now the Americans' ammunition was nearly depleted. As the British began the third assault they were met by two volleys of American fire, but then the colonists' guns fell virtually silent. As the British ascended the hill, they found most of the militiamen had retreated to Bunker Hill, although a handful stayed behind to pick off the advancing Redcoats with sniper fire. One British soldier later complained, "Never had the British Army so ungenerous an enemy to oppose. [The colonists] conceal themselves behind trees . . . till an opportunity presents itself of taking a shot at our advance sentries, which done they immediately retreat. What an unfair method of carrying out a war!"[6]

> "Don't one of you fire until you see the whites of their eyes."[4]
>
> —Colonial militia commander William Prescott.

After three assaults the British took Breed's Hill. The British entered battle with 2,500 troops: 1,054 were killed or wounded. The Americans—losers in the battle—tried to hold Breed's Hill with less than half the men. Their losses totaled a relatively small 144 killed and 271 wounded. Moreover, the Charlestown peninsula hardly held the strategic significance the British had imagined. In March 1776 Howe withdrew his forces from the peninsula, and all of Boston, after colonists rained cannon fire onto their positions. In other words, the British suffered huge casualties to take a worthless piece of land.

A War Fought with Resolve

Breed's Hill was an early battle in a war that would rage for six years. The war was prompted when the British exerted a heavy hand on the colonies, attempting to extract taxes and impose other measures that threatened the colonists' freedom. The colonists reacted by taking up arms and fighting for the right to self-governance and democracy.

Breed's Hill was not a military victory—the battle ended when the colonists retreated, turning over the hill to the British. But it was clearly a moral victory. The British sustained heavy losses in taking the hill, reflecting the nature of the war ahead: A long and bloody conflict, fought with dedicated resolve by the colonists to free themselves from a repressive government that had attempted to rule them from thousands of miles away.

CHAPTER ONE

A Brief History of the American Revolution

The American Revolution was a revolution unlike any other that had occurred throughout history. By the time the American colonies declared their independence from Great Britain in 1776, dozens of insurrections had been waged over the centuries by oppressed peoples in Europe and Asia. Many of those revolutions were unsuccessful, put down by powerful monarchs. But even those that succeeded invariably resulted in the establishment of new monarchies, ruled by kings and queens who maintained autocratic authority over their people.

The American Revolution aimed to create a new society, governed by the people. In the Declaration of Independence Thomas Jefferson spelled out the purpose of the Revolution with these words: "We hold these truths to be self-evident, that all men are created equal, that they are endowed by their Creator with certain unalienable Rights, that among these are Life, Liberty and the pursuit of Happiness.—That to secure these rights, Governments are instituted among Men, deriving their just powers from the consent of the governed."

The Revolution was sparked when the British Parliament and monarch, King George III, attempted to exert more authority over the colonies and, specifically, tax the colonists to pay the British government's debts. The colonists found the taxes repugnant, but their outrage was also focused on the way in which the taxes were assessed: through the dictates of a government sitting in a European capital thousands of miles distant, aloof to the complaints or desires of the colonists. Thomas Paine, the firebrand colonial editor, provided the framework for the Revolution in his January 1776 pamphlet titled *Common Sense*. Paine declared that Great Britain's notion of governance—a monarchy in control of far-off colonies—no longer fit into an emerging modern world. Wrote Paine, "It is repugnant to reason, to the universal order of things to all examples from former ages, to suppose, that this continent can longer remain subject to any external power. . . . The utmost stretch of human wisdom cannot, at this time, compass a plan short of separation."[7]

Fifteen years before the first shots in the Revolution were fired, the American people lived in thirteen separate colonies. They were suspicious of one another, even maintaining navies to ensure each other's merchant ships were not evading tariffs by making late-night runs across rivers. They issued their own currencies and lived under their own laws. But they were loyal to the British king. However, by 1776 leaders of the colonial governments reached the unanimous conclusion that they were better off united and that freedom and self-rule were worth fighting for. And as Paine illustrates in *Common Sense*, they had also concluded that government by a distant monarchy was not an acceptable framework for the future. "The Revolution . . . was an integral part of the great transforming process that carried America into the liberal democratic society of the modern world," says historian Gordon Wood. "The Revolution shattered what remained of these traditional patterns of life and prepared the way for the more fluid, more bristling, individualistic world that followed."[8]

> "It is repugnant to reason, to the universal order of things to all examples from former ages, to suppose, that this continent can longer remain subject to any external power. . . . The utmost stretch of human wisdom cannot, at this time, compass a plan short of separation."[7]
>
> —Colonial editor Thomas Paine.

Roots of the Revolution

The roots of the Revolution were planted in 1760 when British troops, assisted by colonial militias, defeated the French and their Indian allies in the French and Indian War. The war, which broke out in 1754, erupted when French troops attempted to seize control of the Ohio Valley, a major source of trade for the nearby Virginia colony. The French and Indian War was actually the fourth conflict fought between the British and French in the colonies over the course of some sixty years. Each of these wars concerned French efforts to widen their

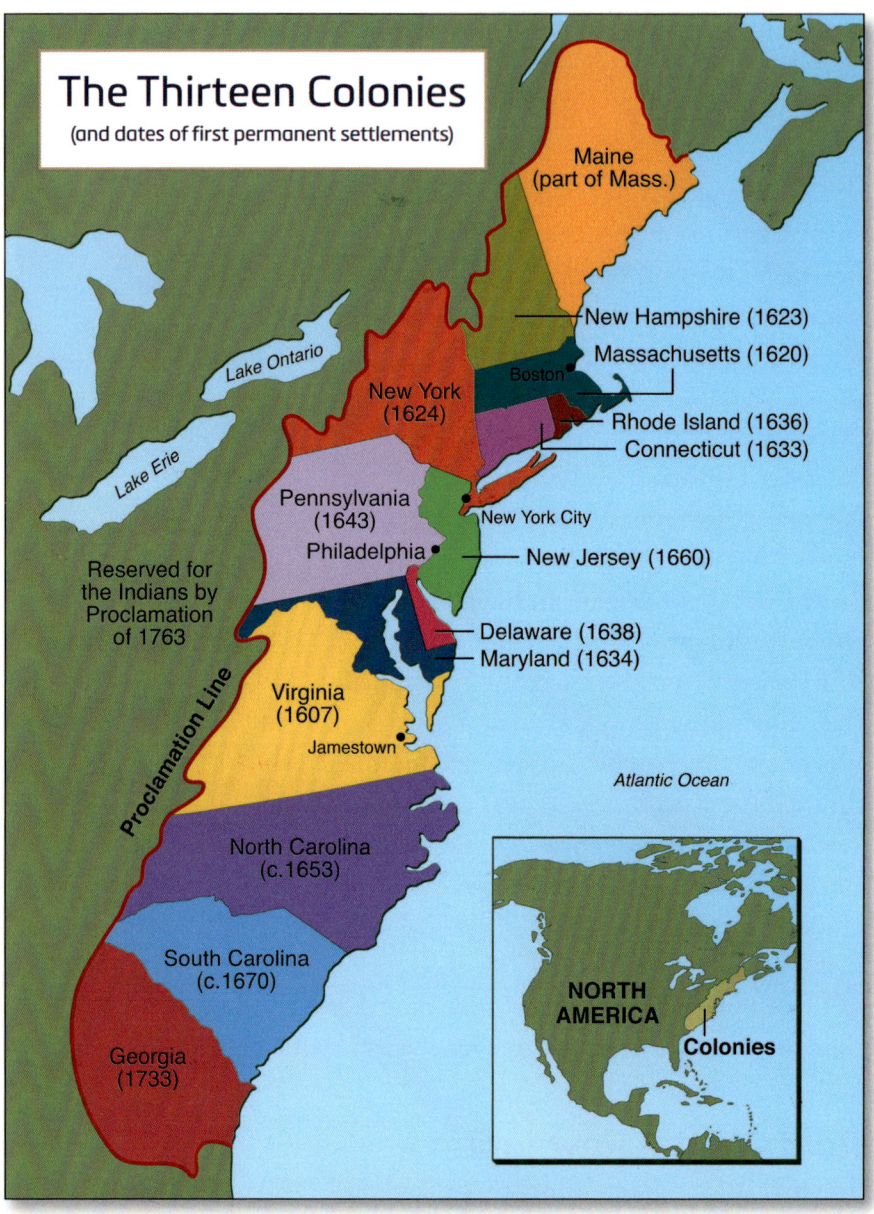

control over the lucrative fur and agricultural trades in the colonies. But the British victory in the French and Indian War put an end to French designs on controlling commerce in the colonies.

Nevertheless, the war had ramifications unseen at first by the British. The British sent troops to America to defend the colonists, but the colonies were also expected to raise militias. They received no financial support from the home country to help them arm the colonial militias, leaving many of the colonial governments in debt. Moreover, with the threat of French attack eliminated, the colonists no longer looked on the king and Parliament as their protectors. Thousands of miles from America, Charles Gravier, French ambassador to the Ottoman Empire, had this to say when he learned of the French defeat: "The colonies will no longer need Britain's protection. She will call on them to contribute toward supporting the burdens they have helped to bring on her, and they will answer by striking off their chains."[9]

Taxing the Colonists

In the decade following the French and Indian War, complaints about British rule surfaced as the British Parliament imposed taxes as well as military authority over the colonies. In 1764 the British imposed the Sugar Act, a tax on molasses, followed a year later by the Stamp Act, assessed on newspapers, legal documents, and even playing cards. The colonies reacted to the Stamp Act by sending delegates to the Stamp Act Congress, where the first complaints against "taxation without representation" were raised. When Parliament ignored the petition by the Stamp Act Congress to repeal the levy, civil disobedience erupted in several colonies. In 1765 a mob in Massachusetts forced the royal tax collector to resign, then burned down the Boston Customs House, the building where taxes were collected. A year later, in response to the violent demonstrations breaking out in the colonies, Parliament repealed the Stamp Act—but passed the Declaratory Act, a law that reinforced Parliament's position that the British government held ultimate authority over the colonies.

> "The colonies will no longer need Britain's protection. She will call on them to contribute toward supporting the burdens they have helped to bring on her, and they will answer by striking off their chains."[9]
>
> —Charles Gravier, French ambassador to the Ottoman Empire.

Meanwhile, the British still needed to pay their debts left over from the French and Indian War. So in 1767 the Parliament passed the Townshend Acts, named for the author of the measures, Charles Townshend, the chancellor of the exchequer (the chief financial officer of the

British government). The Townshend Acts assessed taxes on a number of goods exported to the colonies, among them glass, lead, paint, paper, and tea. And to enforce the Townshend Acts, Parliament sent British troops to the colonies—an act that helped inflame passions against the British. In 1770 these passions came to a boiling point in Boston when British troops fired into a mob of unruly protesters, killing five colonists in an incident known as the Boston Massacre.

Again Parliament's taxes had incited violent protests, and again Parliament found it necessary to repeal the taxes in order to maintain peace. Shortly after the incident in Boston, Parliament repealed all the levies under the Townshend Acts—except the tax on tea, which it left in place as a statement that Parliament still had the power to

A lithograph shows the tarring and feathering of a tax collector working for the British Crown. Colonials staged many such protests to show their displeasure at being taxed without representation in the British Parliament.

make laws and impose taxes in the colonies. In response, the colonists refused to buy British tea and instead obtained tea smuggled from the Netherlands. This act of defiance by the colonists had a devastating effect on the British East India Company, which found itself with few buyers for 18 million pounds of tea stored in its warehouses. In 1773 Parliament passed the Tea Act compelling the colonies to buy British tea. This was the measure that prompted the Boston Tea Party, in which colonists masquerading as Indians boarded three British merchant ships docked in Boston Harbor and dumped crates of tea overboard.

Lexington and Concord

Parliament, now determined to rein in such revolutionary conduct, passed the Coercive Acts—known in the colonies as the Intolerable Acts—stripping the Massachusetts colonial assembly of its power and appointing a military governor to oversee the rebellious colony. In response to Parliament's action, twelve of the thirteen colonies sent delegates to Philadelphia in September 1774 to support the people of Massachusetts and plan a unified response to Parliament's heavy hand. (Georgia initially declined to send a delegate to the Continental Congress. At the time, the colony hoped to enlist British troops to help protect its citizens from attacks by Indian tribes.)

> "Stand your ground. Don't fire unless fired upon. But if they mean to have a war, let it begin here."[10]
>
> —Massachusetts militia captain John Parker.

As the debate in Philadelphia commenced, though, the Massachusetts militia helped sway the argument toward independence when colonial militiamen encountered Redcoats near the town of Lexington on April 19, 1775. At about 4:30 a.m., seventy militiamen stood ready on a meadow near Lexington, awaiting the British approach. Soon they were faced by six companies of Redcoats—believed to number seven hundred men. The militia commander, Captain John Parker, cautioned his men: "Stand your ground. Don't fire unless fired upon. But if they mean to have a war, let it begin here."[10] A few of the colonists, finding themselves outnumbered, murmured that it would be folly to face the British. But Parker ordered them to stand their ground. "The first man who offers to run shall be shot down!"[11] he declared.

The First Shot

A few moments later the British commander, Major John Pitcairn, rode to a point just a hundred feet in front of the colonists' line and ordered them to lay down their arms. Parker ordered his men to fall back, but Pitcairn insisted the colonists drop their weapons. "Damn you!" Pitcairn commanded. "Why don't you lay down your arms?"[12]

A shot was fired. It is unclear whether the first shot of the American Revolution was fired by a colonist or a British soldier. Nevertheless, that shot was followed by volleys from both sides. The initial melee was over in a few minutes—the outnumbered Americans were overrun by the Redcoats. Eight colonists were killed, including Parker. Pitcairn ordered his men to move on to the neighboring town of Concord.

As the Redcoats neared Concord they heard bells ringing. Those bells summoned the town's defenders: militia members, known as Minutemen because they had trained to be ready for battle within a minute's time.

The Redcoats arrived in Concord at about seven o'clock in the morning, finding the town deserted. As they searched Concord the Redcoats set several buildings on fire, sending columns of smoke into the sky. Unknown to the Redcoats, they had committed a disastrous error. The smoke alerted militias in nearby towns that there was trouble in Concord. These neighboring Minutemen quickly mustered and hurried to Concord.

The Minutemen Arrive

The first to arrive were the Minutemen from the neighboring town of Punkatasset Hill. About four hundred members arrived at Concord's North Bridge where they encountered British troops, whom they caught by surprise. The Americans fired into the British ranks, whose members panicked and retreated, falling into chaos as they scattered.

By noon a British colonel, Francis Smith, was able to regroup the Redcoats and, assessing the damage to the ranks, decided to retreat to Boston. About a mile out of town, though, Smith's men encountered heavy concentrations of Minutemen from nearby towns, who had responded to the gun battle they heard in Concord. Over the next sixteen miles the Redcoats were forced to fight their way through a

The Battle of Cowpens

On January 17, 1781, a force of about sixteen hundred men made up of Continental Army troops and members of the Virginia and Georgia militias defeated a British cavalry regiment of about eleven hundred at Cowpens, South Carolina. Historians believe that although the colonists held a small numerical advantage, they won largely because of better leadership. The Americans were led by General Daniel Morgan, the British by Lieutenant Colonel Banastre Tarleton. Morgan was a veteran soldier, having served in the French and Indian War; Tarleton was just twenty-six years old and had a reputation for dash and daring.

During the battle Morgan's men misunderstood a command to redirect their fire, believing they had been ordered to fall back. Seeing what he believed was a retreat, Tarleton ordered his men to rush toward the Americans. Morgan stopped the British advance when he rode into the line and ordered his men to turn and fire. Meanwhile, a nearby reserve unit led by Colonel William Washington saw the British attack and ordered his men to rush the Redcoats. Says historian John Buchanan, "The British regulars collapsed and, in the words of a teenager fighting with the [American] cavalry, 'did the prettiest sort of running.'"

Tarleton suffered overwhelming losses: some eight hundred men killed, wounded, or taken prisoner. The American losses included twenty-four killed, and about one hundred wounded. Asked by his American captors how the Redcoats could have suffered such a devastating defeat, a British prisoner complained, "Nothing better could be expected from troops commanded by a rash, foolish boy."

John Buchanan, "Reporting the Battle of Cowpens," in Todd Andrlik, ed., *Reporting the Revolutionary War*. Naperville, IL: Sourcebooks, 2012, p. 304.

Quoted in John Tebbel, *Turning the World Upside Down: Inside the American Revolution*. New York: Orion, 1993, p. 355.

gauntlet of colonist fire. As the Redcoats traipsed through the woods, they occasionally broke into clearings—where American fire rained down on them. At the town of Cambridge, just north of Boston, the Minutemen finally gave up the chase. The surviving Redcoats limped

The colonial militia engages British regulars on the Lexington common. Although the Redcoats scattered the handful of assembled men and marched to Concord, more than two thousand Minutemen from the surrounding countryside eventually converged on the area and turned the tide of the battle.

into Boston. The final toll from the battle: 273 Redcoats killed, while the Americans lost 95 militiamen.

Lexington and Concord marked the first battle of the American Revolution. The victory by the Minutemen proved colonial militias could stand the test against the British army—regarded as the most powerful fighting force on earth. Still, following Lexington and Concord, the Continental Congress decided the war could not be waged by the colonial militias only. The Congress raised an army of regulars, the Continental Army, placing it under the command of George Washington, a leader of the Virginia militia.

Signing the Declaration of Independence

Many battles followed Lexington and Concord: The Battle of Breed's Hill represented a British victory but at a steep cost. However, an ill-fated strategy by the colonists to draw Canadians into the war on the American side failed when the Continental Army was defeated at the Battle of Quebec. Another British victory followed in the summer of

1776 at the Battle of Brooklyn in New York, also known as the Battle of Long Island.

Even as British forces massed to attack New York, the delegates attending the the Continental Congress believed in their mission. As the attack on New York neared, the delegates meeting in Philadelphia adopted the Declaration of Independence. Authored by Virginia delegate Thomas Jefferson, the Declaration set down in writing the many complaints the colonists held against the king and Parliament. They ranged from unfair taxation to violations of the freedoms the colonists had come to take for granted since the earliest pioneers made the Atlantic crossing nearly two hundred years earlier. On July 2 the Declaration was adopted unanimously by the delegates from the thirteen colonies (by now Georgia had joined the Congress). On July 4 John Hancock, a delegate from Massachusetts who served as president of the Congress, placed his wide and sprawling signature on the Declaration.

Following the Battle of Brooklyn Washington's army retreated into New Jersey, then crossed the Delaware River into Pennsylvania. Although greatly outnumbered, Washington took advantage of a strategic blunder by the British to launch a Christmas night surprise attack at the Battle of Trenton.

Meanwhile, the Philadelphia printer, inventor, and statesman Benjamin Franklin arrived in France as an ambassador with the mission of enlisting Great Britain's longtime enemy into the conflict on the side of the colonists. As Franklin negotiated with the French, another British military blunder in October 1777 left an army under the command of General Burgoyne outnumbered and vulnerable at Saratoga, New York. Burgoyne's surrender convinced the French that the colonists could win the war; and they pledged loans, arms, troops, warships, and military commanders to help defeat their enemy, the British.

Great Britain's Southern Strategy

Still, the war would not be easily won. Following the colonists' victory at Saratoga, the British defeated Washington's troops at two Pennsylvania battles: Brandywine and Germantown, forcing Washington to retreat and make camp for the winter at Valley Forge in the countryside near Philadelphia.

As the weather warmed, and both British and American troops went back on the march, much of the action in the war moved into the southern colonies, where the British attempted a new strategy. The British believed the southern colonists to be more loyal than those in the North and, in fact, were able to organize several loyalist militias. By December the British captured Savannah, Georgia. Victories in Charleston and Camden, South Carolina, followed in 1780. But in October 1780 patriot militias from Virginia, North Carolina, and South Carolina defeated a loyalist militia at Kings Mountain, South Carolina. Three months later, on January 17, 1781, the colonists defeated the British at Cowpens, South Carolina. The victory at Cowpens was a massacre, with virtually the entire British force killed, wounded, or taken prisoner.

Cornwallis Surrenders

Two months after Cowpens the main British force in the South, now under the command of General Lord Charles Cornwallis, fought a bloody but inconclusive battle against the Continental Army at Guilford Courthouse in North Carolina. His ranks thinned and supplies running low, Cornwallis withdrew to Yorktown, Virginia. Located on the banks of the York River, Cornwallis made camp there believing he could receive reinforcements and new provisions from British ships sailing up the river from the Chesapeake Bay. Aiming to attack Cornwallis, Washington, whose army was camped in New Jersey, marched his troops south to Virginia to rendezvous with French troops also arriving by sea.

By late summer Cornwallis's army was continually harassed by Continental army troops and militiamen under the command of a French general, the Marquis de Lafayette. On September 5 a British fleet dispatched with reinforcements for Cornwallis engaged in a sea battle with the French at the Battle of the Capes in the Chesapeake Bay. Unable to run through the French blockade, the British were forced to turn back, leaving Cornwallis with few troops to defend Yorktown. On October 9 American and French troops commenced the siege of Yorktown by raining cannon fire down on British positions. On October 19, 1781, Cornwallis surrendered to Washington.

Corwallis's surrender effectively ended the war. By now the British Parliament had had enough of the American Revolution, resolving that the cost of continuing the war was too steep. Following Yorktown, the British agreed to enter peace negotiations. In September 1783

Winter at Valley Forge

George Washington's army of eleven thousand troops spent the difficult winter of 1777 and 1778 camped at Valley Forge, a rugged portion of the Pennsylvania countryside north of Philadelphia. Everyone was cold, and many of the troops were ill. Food was scarce. Many soldiers deserted. To feed his troops Washington organized foraging expeditions throughout the countryside to gather provisions. Two such parties were led by officers Henry Lee and Anthony Wayne, both of whom proved particularly resourceful when it came to finding food and clothing for the men. "By March [1778] the lean, skeleton-like figures who dragged themselves around Valley Forge began to put on flesh," says historian Robert Middlekauff. "And the flesh was now covered by shirts and breeches."

Moreover, as the weather improved, the men received some much-needed training in soldiering from Friedrich Wilhelm von Steubin, a veteran of the army of Frederick the Great, king of the region of Germany known as Prussia. Asking for no pay, von Steubin offered his services to the Continental Congress, which sent him to Valley Forge to train Washington's men. Von Steubin is credited with turning Washington's army into a disciplined fighting force. Of von Steubin, wrote Continental Army colonel Alexander Scammel, "To see a gentleman dignified with a lieutenant colonel's commission from the great Prussian monarch condescend with a grace peculiar to himself to take under his direction a squad of ten or twelve men in the capacity of a drill sergeant, commands the admiration of both officers and men."

Robert Middlekauff, *The Glorious Course: The American Revolution, 1763–1789*. New York: Oxford University Press, 1982, p. 417.

Quoted in John Tebbel, *Turning the World Upside Down: Inside the American Revolution*. New York: Orion, 1993, p. 237.

American and British diplomats signed the Treaty of Paris, granting independence to the colonies. In the eight years since the first shots were fired at Lexington and Concord, a ragtag band of militiamen and untrained soldiers coalesced into an effective fighting force, able to stand up against the world's most powerful military. Certainly they had help from the French, but they also had a resolve to free themselves from a monarchy and establish a society that, as Jefferson wrote, would draw its powers from the consent of the governed.

CHAPTER TWO

How Did the Actions by the King and Parliament Give Rise to the Revolution?

> **Focus Questions**
> 1. What type of future do you think America would have faced if the colonists abided by the king's Proclamation of 1763 and did not encroach on Indian lands west of the Allegheny Mountains?
> 2. Do you think the British should have acted earlier to quell the civil disobedience that was breaking out in the colonies in the years following the French and Indian War? Would a heavier hand have stifled the fervor for revolution, or brought on the war sooner?
> 3. Do you believe the taxes imposed by Parliament, which were assessed to pay the costs of a war waged to protect the colonists against the French and Indians, could be regarded as fair and justified?

The French and Indian War was actually part of a larger conflict that embroiled Great Britain and France. While British troops and colonial militias fought the French and Indians in the American colonies, the British military was also forced to engage foreign armies on European battlefields. In Great Britain and other European countries the conflict is known more familiarly as the Seven Years' War.

The war started when Austria attacked Prussia, now a region of Germany, over disputed territories. Great Britain allied with Prussia, while Sweden, France, Spain, and Russia came to Austria's defense. The war even spread to India, where Great Britain battled France. The war ended in victory for Prussia and Great Britain. As part of the 1763 Treaty of Paris, large territories in Europe and India were awarded to the Prussians and British—who also prevailed in the American colonies, ousting the French.

Although Great Britain achieved a sweeping triumph in both Europe and America, the victory was costly. During seven years of warfare, the British government spent 122 million pounds—a sum equivalent in twenty-first-century US funds to some $12 billion. Moreover, that money was largely borrowed from British banks; after the war, the British government was responsible for paying 4.4 million pounds a year in interest payments—about $748 million in modern US dollars.

Pushing West of the Allegheny Mountains

To repay these debts the Parliament enacted taxes on the citizens of the British Isles. Wealthy citizens were forced to pay more taxes on the lands they owned. Those who did not own property found themselves paying higher taxes on beer and tobacco. Soon newspapers, sugar, paper, and linen were taxed as well. Eventually, hundreds of goods found in British society were taxed by Parliament. Says historian Robert Middlekauff, "If a man owned a house, he not only paid a tax on it, but on every window in it; if he decided to take the air in his carriage, perhaps fleeing the tax collector, he rode with the depressing knowledge that the carriage too was taxed."[13]

Despite imposing and collecting all manner of new taxes on British citizens, Parliament was still unable to pay the nation's war debts. More revenue was needed by the government, and the money to pay these debts had to come from somewhere. And so to meet its obligations to the British banks, the Parliament looked to the colonies and the imposition of heavy taxes.

In fact, even before the first taxes were imposed on the colonies, King George realized that although the French had signed the treaty, their allies in the colonies—the Indian tribes—had not been represented at the peace negotiations. George worried that the Indians would continue to attack the colonists, forcing the British government to send more troops to America. And so in October 1763—just eight months after signing the Treaty of Paris—George issued the

The Battle of Minden in Prussia in 1759 was a victory for the Anglo-Prussian alliance over the French during the Seven Years' War. Such victories were costly, and American colonists were expected to bear part of Britain's financial burden.

Proclamation of 1763 prohibiting settlement in the colonies west of the Allegheny Mountains. (The range passes through what are now the states of Pennsylvania, Maryland, Virginia, West Virginia, Ohio, and Kentucky.)

Although the Indians were not represented at the Treaty of Paris, following the Seven Years' War the British negotiated several peace treaties with individual Indian tribes, guaranteeing them exclusive use of lands west of the Allegheny Mountains. But these treaties and the king's proclamation infuriated many colonial assemblies, which believed their citizens had the right to push the American frontier west.

And, in fact, many colonial pioneers ignored the Proclamation and explored new lands west of the Allegheny Mountains. The colonial pioneers trapped furs and often tangled with Indians they encountered. The pioneers who encroached on Indian lands were more than just individual backwoodsmen exploring the wilderness to earn meager livings as trappers. They had the support of business leaders in the large colonial cities, one of which was the Illinois Company. A principal in the Illinois Company was Benjamin Franklin, who would go on to play a significant role in the cause for independence. In the 1760s, though, Franklin hoped to earn a considerable profit by opening new lands west of the Allegheny Mountains to colonial settlement so that his company and others could make profits from the fur trade and agricultural potential available in the wilderness.

Taxing the Colonists

The British bristled at such defiance by the colonies but found they could do little to curb the encroachment into Indian lands. Says Middlekauff, "The West had proved virtually ungovernable. Royal officials, most notably the superintendents of Indian Affairs, found themselves helpless to regulate the fur trade and consequently to prevent frauds against the Indians. And settlers defied the ban against settlement and encroached upon lands supposedly reserved to the Indians."[14]

In fact, in the months following the Treaty of Paris Parliament had already decided to keep troops in the colonies, and the cash-strapped British lawmakers had no interest in sending their troops stationed in America into new frontiers. Moreover, to cut costs the British government closed most of its forts. To house the troops, in 1765 the Parliament passed the Quartering Act, requiring colonists to house British soldiers in their homes. Again, this act infuriated many colonists who found themselves hosting and feeding—without compensation—unwanted houseguests.

By then Parliament had enacted the first of several taxes on the colonies to help finance repayment of the huge debt left over from the Seven Years' War. These taxes were imposed under the Sugar Act of 1764, Stamp Act of 1765, and Townshend Acts of 1767. These acts assessed heavy taxes on consumers, merchants, and farmers. The Sugar

> "The West had proved virtually ungovernable. Royal officials, most notably the superintendents of Indian Affairs, found themselves helpless to regulate the fur trade and consequently to prevent frauds against the Indians."[14]
>
> —Historian Robert Middlekauff.

Act imposed taxes on colonial merchants who exported molasses—a tax that was felt by the sugarcane growers because it meant they were offered lower prices for their crops. The Stamp Act assessed levies on newspapers, pamphlets, legal documents, and other publications printed in the colonies. And the Townshend Acts assessed levies on a number of consumer products, among them tea, glass, paper, lead, and paint.

Civil Disobedience

Colonists at first responded with resolutions adopted by their colonial assemblies protesting the taxes, but these acts were largely symbolic since English law still prevailed in the colonies. In 1765 nine of the thirteen colonies sent representatives to the Stamp Act Congress to frame a formal protest against the tax. Although this meeting marks the first time the colonies acted in concert against the British government, the resolution by the Stamp Act Congress was, again, largely symbolic. The colonial governments were virtually powerless to oppose edicts decreed by the king and Parliament.

But colonists showed hostility in other ways. Public demonstrations that included acts of violence broke out in the colonies. Massachusetts was a particular hotbed of unrest against the British government. In 1765 a mob led by Boston shoemaker Ebenezer McIntosh forced England's designated tax collector to quit his job, then demolished the Customs House, the building where British taxes were collected. Finally, McIntosh's mob destroyed the home of the colony's lieutenant governor—an appointee of the king. When the royal governor ordered the sheriff to arrest McIntosh, the sheriff declined—advising the governor that McIntosh's arrest would lead to further violence.

To respond to acts of defiance shown by McIntosh and others, the British Parliament debated the need to send more troops to the colonies. There were those in the Parliament who believed the growing insurrection should be smashed with force. Other members believed that the presence of more troops in the colonies would lead to further unrest, so they coun-

> "There is the most urgent reason to do what is right, and immediately, but what is that right, and who is to do it?"[15]
>
> —William Barrington, British secretary of war.

seled a more moderate approach. In 1767 the British secretary of war, William Barrington, said, "There is the most urgent reason to do what is right, and immediately, but what is that right, and who is to do it?"[15]

The civil disobedience continued. In 1770 a relatively minor incident—the throwing of snowballs at British soldiers—led to widespread violence when the troops fired into the crowd, killing five civilians. This incident is known as the Boston Massacre. And in 1772 a British warship, the *Gaspee*, ran aground off the coast of Rhode Island. About seventy Rhode Island colonists, their faces blackened with soot, rowed out to the disabled ship and boarded the vessel. They shot and wounded the captain, then sent the captain and his crew back to shore. Now in command of the vessel, they set the *Gaspee* ablaze.

As the Crown continued to levy taxes on the colonies, Americans began to view the British soldiers stationed in their towns as occupiers. In 1770, the Boston Massacre revealed how the tensions between the colonists and soldiers could turn into violence.

The Boston Massacre

The Boston Massacre helped fuel passions against British rule, but it also helped establish the American principle that individuals accused of crimes are entitled to fair trials—a principle that was later written into law in the US Constitution. The massacre erupted on March 5, 1770, when a group of rowdy Bostonians taunted eight British soldiers standing guard in front of the Boston Customs House. Soon the Bostonians started pelting the soldiers with garbage. Next, members of the crowed hurled snowballs at the soldiers, further taunting them. Finally, the soldiers—believing their lives were in peril—fired into the crowd, killing five people.

The royal governor, Thomas Hutchinson, ordered the arrests of the soldiers and agreed to try them on murder charges. The soldiers found themselves with unlikely defenders—John Adams and Josiah Quincy, Boston lawyers and radical advocates for independence. But Adams and Quincy also believed the soldiers were entitled to a fair trial. When the trial convened, Adams and Quincy proved to the jury the soldiers had been provoked into fearing for their lives. They won acquittals for six of the eight soldiers, while two were convicted of the lesser charge of manslaughter. Their sentence was branding on the thumbs, after which they were released. Adams, a future US president, said he had no qualms about defending the British soldiers, even though they represented an authority he opposed. He said, "Persons whose lives were at stake ought to have the counsel they prefer."

Quoted in Benson Bobrick, *Angel in the Whirlwind: The Triumph of the American Revolution*. New York: Simon & Schuster, 1997, p. 87.

The Intolerable Acts

Another brazen act of civil disobedience occurred in December 1773 when colonists, dressed as Indians, boarded three British merchant vessels docked in Boston Harbor and tossed British-imported tea overboard. In staging what has become known as the Boston Tea Party, the colonists protested an act by the British Parliament forcing Americans to buy tea from British merchants—and pay a hefty tea tax as well.

Says Gordon Wood, "To the British the Boston Tea Party was the ultimate outrage. Angry officials and many of the politically active people in Great Britain clamored for a punishment that would squarely confront America with the issue of Parliament's right to legislate for the colonies. 'We are now to establish our authority,' Lord North told the [Parliament], 'or give it up entirely.'"[16] Parliament decided to act decisively against such brazen acts of disobedience and the following spring passed the Coercive Acts, known in the colonies as the Intolerable Acts. The new laws essentially stripped the Massachusetts colonial assembly of its power to govern and placed authority in the colony under a military officer.

> "We are now to establish our authority or give it up entirely."[16]
>
> —Lord Frederick North, prime minister of Great Britain.

The Loyalists

The Intolerable Acts led in 1774 to the convening of the First Continental Congress in Philadelphia, in which the colonies sent delegates to plan a course of action against the British. At this point there were still

In 1773, a group of enraged colonists boarded British merchant ships to dump their cargoes of tea into Boston Harbor in protest of a newly levied tea tax. Many of the colonials dressed as Mohawk Indians to disguise themselves and to show that they identified with America, not Britain.

many loyalists in the colonies, and they were represented at the Continental Congress. Even after the battles at Lexington and Concord as well as Breed's Hill, there was hardly unity throughout the colonies or in the Continental Congress for a protracted war or formal declaration of independence. Many loyalists still lived in the colonies—they considered themselves subjects of the British Crown and had no taste for independence. In July 1775 a loyalist delegate to the Congress from Pennsylvania, John Dickinson, won backing to send the Olive Branch Petition to London, recognizing the dominion of Great Britain over the colonies and asking the king to use influence to resolve the differences between the colonies and the mother country.

In February 1776 the Parliament issued its response to the Olive Branch Petition. Instead of seeking a peaceful end to their differences, Parliament enacted the Prohibitory Act, authorizing the British navy to attack merchant vessels attempting to enter American ports. The act was a clear effort by the British government to cut off raw materials—as well as arms and ammunition—shipped to the colonies by Great Britain's European enemies. The Prohibitory Act helped turn many loyalists in the Continental Congress into advocates for independence. Said delegate Joseph Hewes of North Carolina, a longtime loyalist, "Nothing is left now but to fight it out."[17]

> "Nothing is left now but to fight it out."[17]
>
> —Joseph Hewes, delegate to the Continental Congress.

Debate in Philadelphia

The most intense debate on independence occurred in May and June of 1776, during which a string of events led the remaining loyalists in the Continental Congress to finally concede they had no option other than to join the fight. At first, the independence movement suffered a setback when on May 1 Pennsylvanians voted to send a pro-loyalist majority to the colonial assembly. Pennsylvania was the largest and most influential colony in America, but unlike the other colonies it did not fall directly under the authority of the king. Under the original charter granted by the British monarchy a century earlier to the colony's founder, William Penn, the Penn family—and not the king and Parliament—held most of the authority in the colony. As such, many Pennsylvanians did not feel threatened by the British.

Benjamin Franklin in London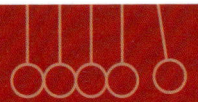

Although civil disobedience was a tactic employed by the colonists, political leaders in the colonies did make attempts at diplomacy. Arriving in 1765, Benjamin Franklin spent a decade in Great Britain, appearing before Parliament several times.

As the Parliament applied taxes and other measures of its authority over the colonies, Franklin found himself trying to convince British lawmakers that their actions were unfair and burdensome. In response, Franklin was berated by British lawmakers, who demanded to know why the colonies refused to follow British law.

"No middle doctrine can be well maintained," Franklin said in 1766, after a frustrating appearance before Parliament. "Something might be made of either of the extremes; that Parliament has a power to make all the laws for us, or that it has a power to make no laws for us." As Franklin spent more time in London, he found himself increasingly drawn to the argument that Parliament should have no power to make laws for the colonies. In 1775 Franklin left London and returned to his home in Philadelphia, dedicated to the cause for independence.

Quoted in Gordon S. Wood, *The Americanization of Benjamin Franklin*. New York: Penguin, 2004, p. 124.

But that attitude started changing a week later when news reached the colonies that King George had had enough of the insurrection and aimed to end it quickly. The king hired mercenaries from a region of Germany known as Hess, dispatching them to the colonies, including Pennsylvania, to deal harshly with the upstart colonists and their militias. And on May 8 a British warship, the *Roebuck*, was sighted by sentries as it sailed up the Delaware River toward Philadelphia. Suspecting the mission of the *Roebuck* was to bombard the city with cannon shells, Pennsylvania militiamen quickly mustered and boarded small boats. They rowed out to engage the *Roebuck* and, after a daylong battle, succeeded in disabling the warship. Since the battle occurred a mile from Philadelphia, it sent a strong message to the Pennsylvania loyalists that they were not immune from the wrath of the British.

By now debate was well under way in the Continental Congress, where delegates considered petitions for independence. Leading the debate for independence was the Massachusetts delegate John Adams, whose persuasive rhetoric helped overcome whatever loyalist sympathies remained in the Congress. Outside the State House the working people of Pennsylvania—those who had been sending their sons into the local militias—rallied in support of independence, staging boisterous demonstrations calling for war. On June 9 news reached the Congress that a huge fleet of British warships had been dispatched from Nova Scotia in Canada with the intention of laying siege to the city of New York.

Jefferson Drafts the Declaration of Independence

Two days before news of the impending British attack on New York reached Philadelphia, the Congress appointed a Committee of Five to draft the Declaration of Independence. Jefferson was named chairman of the Committee and assumed the responsibility to draft the Declaration.

Historians believe the Declaration was completed in the third week of June 1776. Over the next two weeks the delegates debated its language, making deletions and additions to the document but leaving most of the message intact. On July 2 the delegates voted to accept the Declaration. On July 4, a delegate from Massachusetts—John Hancock, the president of the Continental Congress—placed his signature on the 1,337-word document. Over the course of the next few months the other delegates added their names as well.

United Against a Common Foe

To quell dissent and put down the many acts of civil disobedience, the British took measures they felt they had to take: They enhanced their military presence and used the power of Parliament to adopt the Intolerable Acts, sending what they believed were clear messages that

Great Britain's rule over the colonies would endure. These measures served only to inflame the colonists' passions against British rule. They helped unite the colonists against a common foe, Great Britain, which ultimately led to a call for independence.

Leaders of the thirteen colonies resolved they could no longer live under the rule of Great Britain. In the end, the British were forced to do what they sought to avoid since the end of the French and Indian War. They had to send more troops and incur even more debt to maintain order in a part of the world where their influence had waned and their authority was no longer wanted.

CHAPTER THREE

How Did the Battles of Trenton and Princeton Change the Course of the Revolution?

Focus Questions

1. How did George Washington's triumphs at Trenton and Princeton influence American morale? How important was this in the overall course of the war?
2. How did British attitudes toward their American adversaries affect the outcomes of important battles?
3. What do you think is the message of Thomas Paine's *An American Crisis?*

By the summer of 1776 the colonists' desire to wage war against the British was far from resolute. Despite the military victory at Lexington and Concord and the moral victory at Breed's Hill, the war soon took a harsh turn against the colonists. In late 1775 the Continental Army traveled north in a campaign to drive the British out of Canada and enlist the Canadians in the cause of independence. On December 31 American forces laid siege to Quebec City. But the Continental Army suffered heavy losses and was forced to retreat.

The defeat at the Battle of Quebec filled many colonists with doubts about the likelihood of success for their cause. Many of those who harbored misgivings were serving in the Continental Army and colonial militias. Between 1775 and 1776 the Continental Army and colonial militias suffered widespread desertions, as many men chose to return to their farms or trades. Says historian Graeme Kent, "Many were fed up with the low pay and alternate boredom and dangers of a soldier's life. Others were homesick; many farmers felt they had to get home to harvest their crops before their families starved."[18]

In fact, desertions became such a problem that Congress offered a bounty of thirty dollars for each deserter returned to the ranks. However, George Washington did not have enough troops to send home to arrest deserters, and so he was forced to suffer a steady decline in troop strength. Miles away from Philadelphia, where the Continental Congress debated the Declaration of Independence, the course of the war had turned bleak. Prospects for victory, even after the Declaration's adoption, seemed a distant possibility until Washington achieved two rousing victories that encouraged and emboldened his troops.

British Advance on New York

On June 29, 1776, as the Continental Congress in Philadelphia prepared to vote on the Declaration of Independence, New Yorker Daniel McCurtin woke in his seaside home to discover a most unusual sight. The Lower Bay, a part of the Atlantic Ocean that washes against Staten Island and Manhattan, was filled with British warships. He said, "I . . . spied as I peeped out . . . something resembling a wood of pine trees trimmed . . . the whole Bay was full of shipping as ever it could be. I . . . thought all London was afloat."[19]

The colonists had known of the British advance on New York for weeks. News of the dispatch of the fleet from Nova Scotia helped convince many loyalist delegates in the Congress to support independence. As McCurtin's eyewitness account illustrates, by late June the fleet had arrived. Moreover, British troops occupied Staten Island and areas of northern New Jersey. And colonial scouts saw the decks of the ships anchored in the Lower Bay carried not only soldiers wearing the red coats of the British army but soldiers wearing brass helmets and blue coats as well. These were the Hessian mercenaries from Germany King George had summoned. "So the stage is set for a great battle, first of the war," says historian John Tebbel. "The British have already flexed their muscles, insolently sailing up the Hudson [River] past the shore batteries, just to prove

> "I . . . spied as I peeped out . . . something resembling a wood of pine trees trimmed . . . the whole Bay was full of shipping as ever it could be. I . . . thought all London was afloat."[19]
>
> —New Yorker Daniel McCurtin.

they can do it, letting go a few broadsides as they pass, which sends New York into a state of panic."[20]

The Battle of Brooklyn

By August still more British ships anchored off the coast of New York. Washington made plans to defend the city, stationing troops in Manhattan and on Long Island. On August 22 eighty-eight barges filled with Redcoats and Hessians left the anchored ships. By the end of the day some thirty-two thousand British and Hessian troops had set foot in New York. Washington's army was greatly outnumbered—just some seventeen thousand Continental soldiers and local militiamen had been mustered for the battle.

The British found their adversaries laughably ill-prepared for what awaited them. British naval officer Ambrose Serle eyed the American troops facing the Redcoats and Hessians and provided this description: "The strangest that was ever collected: Old men of 60, Boys of 14 ... ragged for the most part, compose the motley Crew."[21]

On the night of August 26, 1776, the British opened fire. Redcoats and Hessians easily overran American positions in the Brooklyn area of New York. The survivors escaped into nearby marshes. The British and Hessians pursued, looting and setting fire to farmhouses and village homes they encountered along the rural routes leading out of the city. Croplands were set afire as well. After the first day of fighting, more than one thousand Americans were dead, wounded, or captured.

Washington's men had retreated into Brooklyn and now found themselves with the East River at their backs. As Washington dug in, the British and Hessians formed a semicircle around his position. Washington fully expected British ships to sail up the East River, thus completely surrounding his camp.

The weather came to Washington's rescue. A storm swept through the New York area, preventing the British ships from moving up the East River. Following the storm, a heavy fog fell over the river. Unknown to the British, Washington summoned hundreds of fishermen from Cape Cod near Boston, who arrived at the American encampment on the East River and, under the shroud of fog, ferried the entire army to safety.

Still, there was no denying the Battle of Brooklyn, also known as the Battle of Long Island, represented a tremendous loss for the colonists. More than three thousand colonists died in the battle; the Hessians lost about three hundred men, while the British regulars lost no more than fifty. Washington knew that beyond the loss of troops, the outcome of the battle had a devastating impact on the morale of the troops and public support for the cause. "Our situation is truly distressing," he said after the battle.

> The . . . [defeat] our detachment sustained . . . has dispirited too great a proportion of our troops and filled their minds with apprehension and despair. The militia, instead of calling forth their utmost efforts to a brave and manly opposition in order to repair our losses, are dismayed, intractable, and impatient to return [home]. Great numbers of them have gone off; in some instances, almost whole regiments.[22]

A modern painting of the Delaware Regiment at the Battle of Brooklyn. Although most of the colonial troops were dressed in a variety of outfits, the Delaware uniform of a blue jacket over white waistcoat and breeches would become the standard for the newly modernizing Continental Army.

Washington's Dispirited Troops

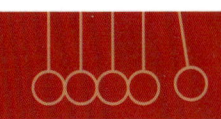

Following the Battle of Brooklyn (also known as the Battle of Long Island), the colonists came close to losing the war because of an erosion in troop strength. Dispirited by the loss, soldiers left the Continental Army and their colonial militias in droves. Many left when their enlistments expired, refusing to reenlist. Some deserted. Historian John Tebbel describes these events: "In the aftermath of Long Island, morale has never been lower. A good many of the militia are beginning to think of the war as a bad thing, and they're getting out of it. [George Washington] reports despairingly to Congress that they're leaving 'almost by whole regiments.'"

Congress tried to shore up the ranks. Shortly after the Battle of Brooklyn, Congress authorized the recruitment of eighty thousand new troops for the Continental Army. But since Congress had few resources to organize the recruitment, it asked the colonial assemblies to head efforts within their colonies to find new troops. The assemblies were slow to respond. Says historian Robert Middlekauff, "The . . . legislatures acted slowly, or rather did nothing at all for several months, and the authorized regiments went unfilled while Washington begged for troops."

Not until Washington achieved decisive victories at the battles of Trenton and Princeton did recruitment pick up, finally providing Washington with the troops he needed to continue the Revolution. Prior to the battles of Trenton and Princeton, Washington is believed to have had just five thousand troops under his command. By the end of 1777 that number had grown to nearly thirty-seven thousand.

John Tebbel, *Turning the World Upside Down: Inside the American Revolution.* New York: Orion, 1993, p. 135.

Robert Middlekauff, *The Glorious Course: The American Revolution, 1763–1789.* New York: Oxford University Press, 1982, p. 350.

Washington's Retreat

The pace of desertion Washington's army felt prior to the Battle of Brooklyn now quickened. Nevertheless, others took strength from the defeat, calling on the colonists to use the outcome of the battle to unite. Said Abigail Adams, wife of Continental Congress delegate and future president John Adams, "But if we should be defeated, I think we shall not be conquered. A people fired, like the Romans, with love of their country and of liberty, a zeal for the public good, and a noble emulation of glory, will not be disheartened or dispirited by a succession of unfortunate events. But, like them, may we learn the power of becoming invincible!"[23]

Following the defeat in Brooklyn, Washington's men spent the next three months in retreat as they headed first north into the New York colony, then turned south, entering New Jersey. They were pursued by two British armies—one led by General William Howe, the other by General Charles Cornwallis. Minor skirmishes were fought along the way, and in each case Washington failed to slow the advance of the superior British forces. During these weeks Fort Washington in New York fell to the British as did Fort Lee in New Jersey. On November 28 Washington camped in New Brunswick, New Jersey—and lost two thousand militiamen from New Jersey and Maryland whose enlistments expired. Instead of reenlisting to continue the fight, the militiamen went home.

On December 3 Washington's dispirited army reached Trenton and made camp. By now the armies led by Howe and Cornwallis had joined into a single force of some ten thousand men. On December 7 they arrived at Washington's camp to find it deserted. The Americans had crossed the Delaware River and were now camped on the Pennsylvania side. Making camp near the village of Taylorsville, Washington commanded an army of just some five thousand men.

And the enlistments of most of those men were due to expire on December 31. Given the heavy air of defeat that had fallen over the men, Washington fully expected most of them to depart the ranks—leaving him with an army of just fourteen hundred troops. Writing to the Continental Congress on December 20, Washington said, "Ten days more will put an end to the existence of our army."[24]

Christmas Night Crossing

The British made camp along a seventy-seven mile front that extended north through New Jersey, ending near the New York border. They left a fifteen-hundred-man regiment of Hessians stationed in Trenton—the southernmost point of the British line. Washington was both shocked and elated when scouts reported the British positions.

The Battle of Trenton, 1776

After making the treacherous journey across the Delaware River, the Continental Army marched to Trenton, New Jersey, where it began its charge on the morning of December 26, 1776. General George Washington led the middle charge. Other units that marched on Trenton moved into position to the west and to the east. Eventually the Continental Army overpowered the Hessians, who were forced to surrender.

American
- ① Continental Army commander in chief George Washington
- ② Major General Nathanael Greene
- ③ Major General John Sullivan
- ④ Brigadier General Hugh Mercer

Hessian

Given the length of the British line, the enemy troops were thinly deployed. Mustering them into an effective strike force would take days if not weeks.

Washington planned a surprise attack on the Hessian camp at Trenton—knowing he outnumbered the German mercenaries and the battle would be over long before British reinforcements could be summoned. Moreover, Washington's scouts reported the Hessian camp was virtually undefended: The Hessian commander, Colonel Johann Rall, failed to fortify the camp with trenches or redoubts.

Washington planned to send twenty-four hundred men across the Delaware River in flat-bottomed barges, landing eight miles north of the Hessians. Once on the New Jersey side the strike force would march south, then encircle the Hessians. The crossing was planned for Christmas night—a time, Washington believed, when the Hessians would be sleeping off the effects of the libations they had consumed during their holiday celebrations.

Trying Times

As the hour for departure neared, Washington assembled his men on the banks of the Delaware River. Before embarking across the river he ordered his officers to read an essay that had been published by Thomas Paine, the firebrand pro-independence editor. Titled *An American Crisis*, Washington's men heard these words before launching the attack on the Hessians:

> "These are the times that try men's souls; the summer soldier and the sunshine patriot will, in this crisis, shrink from the service of his country; but he that stands it now, deserves the love and thanks of man and woman."[25]
>
> —Thomas Paine, from his essay *An American Crisis*.

> These are the times that try men's souls; the summer soldier and the sunshine patriot will, in this crisis, shrink from the service of his country; but he that stands it now, deserves the love and thanks of man and woman. Tyranny, like hell, is not easily conquered; yet we have this consolation with us, that the harder the conflict, the more glorious the triumph.[25]

It was a bitterly cold night, forcing the barges to navigate across the Delaware clashing through chunks of ice. "It will be a terrible night for the soldiers," wrote one officer of the Continental Army, imagining the march ahead, "but I have not heard a man complain."[26]

The crossing commenced just before sunset. The weather favored Washington as clouds covered the moon, providing a veil of darkness over the river. Sleet began falling. Horses and ammunition were ferried across the river as well. By three o'clock in the morning the crossing had been completed.

A Battle Brief but Bloody

The march through the New Jersey woods took five hours. Just north of the Hessian camp the troops encountered a man chopping wood. Captain Thomas Forrest asked the man if he knew the location of the Hessian camp. The man denied knowing. When Forrest motioned to another officer, identifying the officer as Washington, the man exclaimed, "God bless and prosper you, Sir!"[27] The wood chopper then pointed in the direction of the Hessian camp.

The attack commenced. As Washington suspected, the Hessians were sleeping off their Christmas celebrations and were in no condition to repel an attack. Only at the last minute, as Washington's troops fell on the Hessian camp, did the Americans hear shouts from Hessian sentries: "*Der Feind! Heraus! Heraus!* (The enemy! On your feet! On your feet!)"[28]

> "I threw a body of troops in their way, which immediately checked them. Finding, from our disposition, that they were surrounded, and they must inevitably be cut to pieces, if they made any further resistance, they agreed to lay down their arms."[30]
>
> —George Washington, Continental Army commander in chief.

Chaos swept through the camp as the Germans scrambled to find and load their muskets but were invariably shot dead before even lifting them to take aim. Rall managed to muster a group of cavalry soldiers who mounted their horses, making a futile charge. "All my grenadiers forward!"[29] he commanded. But Rall's horsemen were mowed down by colonist fire—Rall was hit twice and mortally wounded.

Washington rode throughout the Hessian camp directing his troops as musket balls whizzed by him. Later, Washington wrote a letter to a Baltimore newspaper, the *Continental Journal*, describing the battle. Of the Hessian mercenaries, he wrote,

> From their motions, they seemed undetermined how to act. Being hard pressed by our troops, who had already got pos-

Hessian mercenary leader Colonel Johann Rall, wounded by colonial fire, surrendered his forces to George Washington at the Battle of Trenton. The remarkable victory roused American spirits throughout the colonies. Shortly after surrendering Rall died from his wounds.

session of part of their artillery, they attempted to file off by a road, on their right ... but perceiving their intention, I threw a body of troops in their way, which immediately checked them. Finding, from our disposition, that they were surrounded, and they must inevitably be cut to pieces, if they made any further resistance, they agreed to lay down their arms.[30]

After two hours the battle was over. Some five hundred of the Hessian mercenaries had been killed and another thousand taken prisoner, many with gunshot wounds. The American losses: three dead, six wounded.

Ten-Dollar Bonuses
Learning of the catastrophe, Cornwallis, at the head of an army of eight thousand Redcoats, hurried toward Trenton, arriving on January 2, 1777. But he had to fight his way south to Trenton because

The British Press Tells Its Version of Events

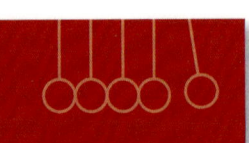

When news of the defeats at the battles of Trenton and Princeton reached London, the British press reacted with disdain—suggesting that George Washington's troops were still no match for the Redcoats. A March 4, 1777, story in the *London Chronicle* even suggests that the British had won the Battle of Princeton:

> The most distinguished encounter occurred . . . near Prince-town. The 17th regiment, consisting of less than 300 men fell in with the rebel army of very superior force, whom they attacked with all the ardour and intrepidity of Britons. They received the fire from behind a fence, over which they immediately leaped upon their enemies, who presently turned to the right about with such precipitation as to leave their very cannon behind them. The soldiers instantly turned their cannon, and fired at least twenty rounds upon their rear, and had they been assisted with another regiment or two, the rebels would have found it rather difficult to make good their retreat. This has been one of the most splendid actions of the whole campaign, and has given a convincing proof that British valour has not declined from its ancient glory.

Quoted in Todd Andrlik, ed., *Reporting the Revolutionary War*. Naperville, IL: Sourcebooks, 2012, p. 214.

Washington stationed snipers in New Jersey, who easily picked off the British troops. Cornwallis finally made camp in Trenton and resolved to attack Washington's troops.

Once again Washington planned to catch the enemy sleeping. Instead of waiting for Cornwallis to launch the attack, Washington struck first—targeting a British encampment at the nearby town of Princeton. On January 3 he encircled the Redcoats and opened fire. The Redcoats retreated into the woods, and Washington's men gave chase. "It's a fine fox chase, my boys!"[31] Washington shouted as his men hunted down the British soldiers.

The victories at Trenton and Princeton were reported in colonial newspapers, raising morale among the colonists and prompting young men to enlist in the Continental Army and colonial militias. Encouraged by the outcomes at Trenton and Princeton, many of Washington's men elected to stay in the army, signing up for new enlistments. News of the victories at Trenton and Princeton had also reached Philadelphia, where the Continental Congress was in session. To encourage the troops to remain with Washington, the Congress voted to award each man who reenlisted a bonus of ten dollars, a generous sum in the colonial era. Says historian Bruce Chadwick, "Following his surprising two victories in ten days, George Washington realized that his army might win the war and that the public would now flock to its cause."[32]

Military and Moral Victories

The losses at Trenton and Princeton represented major blows to the British military mission—in response to the two defeats the British withdrew virtually all their forces from New Jersey, making winter camp in New York. New Jersey had been regarded by the British as a hotbed of loyalism, with many citizens providing aid and reconnaissance to Cornwallis's troops, but now the British were forced to fight in hostile territory. On January 5, 1777, the surgeon James Thacher, traveling with Washington's army, wrote in his journal, "It is now announced in our general orders, to our inexpressible joy and satisfaction, that the scene is in some degree changed, the fortune of war is reversed, and Providence has been pleased to crown the efforts of our commander-in-chief with a splendid victory."[33]

> "The fortune of war is reversed, and Providence has been pleased to crown the efforts of our commander-in-chief with a splendid victory."[33]
>
> —Continental Army surgeon James Thacher.

The colonists won an easy victory at Lexington and Concord, then made the British pay deeply to take Breed's Hill. But the battles of Quebec and Brooklyn had dispirited many soldiers, making them question whether Washington could wage a successful war against the Redcoats. Washington's victories at Trenton and Princeton were not only military victories for the colonists but moral victories as well, proving that they could face, and vanquish, a formidable enemy.

CHAPTER FOUR

How Did Assistance from France Help the American Cause?

> **Focus Questions**
> 1. What do you think would have occurred if the Continental Congress had levied taxes on the American people to finance the Revolution?
> 2. Why was it important for the colonies to obtain a treaty and official recognition from France when the French seemed willing to secretly help the American cause with arms and financial aid?
> 3. How might the Revolution have progressed without French money, arms, and advisers?

On October 26, 1776, seventy-year-old Benjamin Franklin stepped aboard the ship *Reprisal*, which was anchored south of Philadelphia near the small Pennsylvania town of Marcus Hook. The *Reprisal* was about to embark on an important mission. A former merchant ship named *Molly*, the vessel had been purchased the previous spring by the Continental Congress, converted into a warship, and given its new name. The *Reprisal*, in fact, was the first ship in what would become the US Navy. Its mission: to deliver Franklin to France.

Franklin's mission was secret. He boarded the ship at Marcus Hook to throw British spies off his trail. In the previous month the Continental Congress appointed Franklin to head a diplomatic mission to France with the goal of convincing the French to provide aid to the colonies in the war against the British. The colonies were in desperate need of money, arms, ammunition, and military assistance. Knowing of France's longtime hostility toward Great Britain, colonial leaders believed the French could be convinced to assist—in fact, by the time Franklin sailed for France they were already smuggling arms and money to the colonists.

In June 1776, even before the Continental Congress voted on the Declaration of Independence, the French physician Barbeu Dubourg had been appointed by his government as a secret intermediary to smuggle guns to the colonies. Soon after his appointment Dubourg

As the first colonial ambassador, Benjamin Franklin sailed to France to negotiate an alliance against Britain. The French court was charmed by Franklin's wit and humility, but it was also eager to strike back at England for France's defeat in the Seven Years' War.

arranged for the shipment of fifteen thousand French rifles to the colonies. "I hope you brave warriors like these rifles,"[34] wrote Dubourg in a letter to Franklin, adding that he was also working on procuring some cannons for the colonists.

> "I hope you brave warriors like these rifles."[34]
> —Barbeu Dubourg, French physician and secret intermediary to the colonies.

But the Americans needed much more. At the time Franklin was appointed to the diplomatic mission, Washington's troops had just escaped annihilation at the Battle of Brooklyn. The general's first significant victory at Trenton was still months in the future. Even before the Declaration of Independence was signed, there was grave concern in Congress about the colonists' ability to wage a war against what was then the most powerful military on earth.

Worthless Continentals

There was good cause for this concern: In 1776 the entire wealth in the colonies amounted to a mere $12 million, most of it in gold and none held by Congress. The Continental Congress had voted to raise an army, but it had no national treasury, nor did it possess the power to tax the citizens to pay the soldiers—or buy them uniforms, boots, guns, ammunition, or food to feed them. Even if Congress held the power to tax, it lacked the political will to tax. A major cause of the war was the excessive taxation imposed on the colonies by the British. Few members of Congress supported the notion of taxing the colonists—even for a good cause. Says historian Charles Rappleye, "In a war being fought expressly to defy the taxing authority of Parliament, the idea of revolutionary governments imposing heavy domestic taxes was anathema."[35]

And so to pay for the war the Congress simply printed money. But by printing money with no power to tax, Congress solved an immediate problem of raising cash but created the long-term financial problem known as inflation. Since the cash has no real value to begin with, the more cash that is printed, the less it will buy. Over the course of the war the Congress printed money known as "continentals" with face values totaling some $41 million. Whenever Congress needed more money to buy equipment or provisions for the troops, it would print more continentals. As the war dragged on, more and more merchants who were being asked to supply the troops came to regard the continentals as worthless. They stopped accepting them and, therefore, stopped supplying the troops. In 1789 Washington recalled the impact the worthless continentals had on his ability to wage war. "We had no preparation," he said. "Money, the nerve of war, was wanting."[36]

Longtime Enemies

But Great Britain's longtime enemy, France, had the resources to wage war—and it was Franklin's mission to convince the French to aid the

The Thanksgiving of 1777

Starting in 1778 the French government made loans to the Continental Congress totaling $2 million (about $50 million in twenty-first-century dollars). Prior to France's agreement to provide aid to the Revolution, the Congress found it difficult to equip the troops, pay their salaries, or even feed the men. One Continental Army soldier, Joseph Plumb Martin, said it was not unusual for troops to go days without a meal. Martin recalled that for the Thanksgiving holiday of 1777 the Continental Congress ordered that all troops enjoy a feast. Keeping his sense of humor, Martin recounts in his memoir the Thanksgiving "feast" of 1777:

> We had nothing to eat for two or three days previous, except what the trees of the fields and forests afforded us. But we must now have what Congress said—a sumptuous thanksgiving to close the year of high living, we had now nearly seen brought to a close. Well—to add something extraordinary to our present stock of provisions our country, ever mindful of its suffering army, opened her sympathizing heart so wide, upon this occasion, as to give us something to make the world stare. And what do you think that it was, reader? . . . I will tell you: it gave each and every man half a [cup] of rice and a table spoon full of vinegar!

Joseph Plumb Martin, *Memoir of a Revolutionary Soldier: The Narrative of Joseph Plumb Martin*. Mineola, NY: Dover, 2006, p. 57.

American cause. Hostility between the French and British did not begin with the outbreak of the French and Indian War, nor did it end with the 1763 signing of the Treaty of Paris. In fact, the two European monarchies had been in all but perpetual warfare since the eleventh century when the Normans, a French-speaking people under the rule of William the Conqueror, crossed the English Channel and invaded the British Isles. Many wars between the British and French followed, most notably the Hundred Years' War, from 1337 to 1453, in which the French forced English invaders to flee France. This was the conflict in which Joan of Arc emerged as a national heroine by leading a victory over the English at the Battle of Orléans. In 1534 the dispute between the two nations took on a religious element when the British king, Henry VIII, established the Church of England. Henry made the church the predominant faith in Great Britain; British subjects who remained Catholics were persecuted—a circumstance that the Catholic people of France found abhorrent.

> "We had no preparation. Money, the nerve of war, was wanting."[36]
>
> —George Washington.

And so, even though the French suffered defeat in the Seven Years' War, the hostility between the two monarchies was very much on the minds of King George and Lord North—even as their troops defeated Washington at the Battle of Brooklyn. Leaders of the British government were well aware that the insurrection in the colonies was being watched closely by their longtime enemies, and they fully expected the French to enter the war on the colonists' side. They had good reason for these concerns. In composing the Declaration of Independence, Jefferson had used strong language that historians believe was meant specifically to send a message to the French—that the colonists shared their hatred for the British. Reads the Declaration, "The history of the present King of Great Britain is a history of repeated injuries and usurpations, all having in direct object the establishment of an absolute Tyranny over these States."

In 1429, Joan of Arc led the Siege of Orléans, France, a victory that paved the way for Charles VII to reclaim France from partial British rule. Her patriotism and allegiance to the Catholic Church symbolize the deep divide between France and England that persisted through the 1770s.

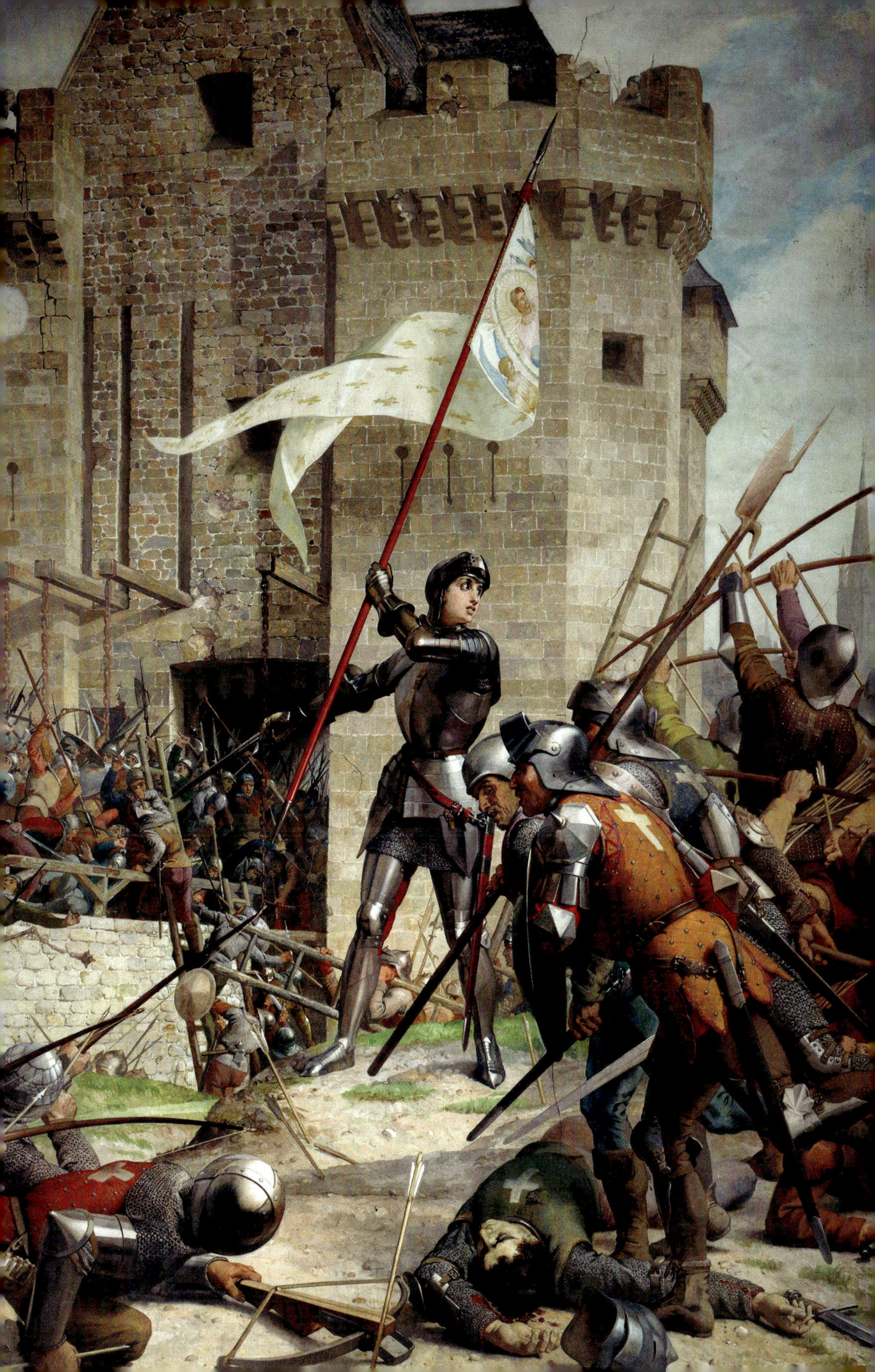

Franklin Arrives in France

Franklin arrived in France in early December after spending a month aboard a ship rocked by frequent bad weather and choppy sailing. So ill from the voyage, the seventy-year-old diplomat had to first rest at an inn in the coastal town of Auray before making the overland trip to Paris. After resting for a few weeks Franklin rode by coach to the French capital, arriving on December 21, 1776.

Franklin knew the future of the Revolution depended on convincing the French to aid the colonies. He started by penning essays that were published in French newspapers, calling attention to the American cause. (A clerk in the French diplomatic service provided the translations.) Working through diplomatic channels, he also convinced the French to continue making surreptitious arms shipments to the colonies. Franklin's allies in the French diplomatic service convinced Spain to provide similar help.

Events at home helped Franklin's campaign. Soon after Washington's success at the battles of Trenton and Princeton, French king Louis XVI agreed to open his country's ports to American privateers. Essentially pirates, these captains and their ships obtained goods in France then made their way through British blockades, supplying the Continental Army with provisions. Also, Louis agreed to secretly send some French army officers across the Atlantic as well to serve as advisers to Washington. (They were appalled by what they found. Upon surveying Washington's troops, one French officer scoffed at the Continental Army, describing the colonists as: "A contemptible band of vagrants, deserters and thieves."[37])

> "A contemptible band of vagrants, deserters and thieves."[37]
>
> —An anonymous French officer's description of American troops.

Louis Hesitates

But Franklin wanted more. He called on Louis to make a full commitment to the American cause: to sign a treaty recognizing American independence and provide overt aid in the form of substantial loans as well as arms, troops, and seasoned commanders.

Franklin knew Louis desired to assist the American colonies for reasons that went beyond France's long-standing hostility toward the

British or a need to avenge the defeat in the Seven Years' War. Franklin made the case that if Great Britain lost its American colonies, the British would lose an important source of wealth, crops, and raw materials. The loss of the colonies would surely weaken the British. Great Britain would be "reduced to that state of weakness and humiliation which she has, by her perfidy, her insolence and her cruelty, both in the east and in the west, so justly merited,"[38] he wrote in a letter to Charles Gravier, now the French foreign minister.

However, if the colonists lost the war, Franklin suggested, then France would find itself facing a much more formidable enemy. The British navy would control the coast of North America and South America. France still had colonies in the Caribbean and South America. Franklin contended that once the British navy was freed of responsibility for putting down the insurrection in America, its might would be loosed on France's colonies in the West.

Louis was pressed to recognize American independence by Gravier, who was convinced the British would be severely weakened by the loss of the colonies. Moreover, he believed he could enlist Spain and Holland—also longtime adversaries of the British—into entering the war as well. Like France, these countries maintained colonies in the West and feared that a strengthened British navy could wrest those colonies from their dominion.

But Louis declined at first to enter a full alliance with the colonists. He was just twenty-two years old when Franklin arrived in France. As a young king he was inexperienced in matters of diplomacy. He also feared war with Great Britain—France had, after all, lost its last conflict with the British. Moreover, as a monarch, Louis's emotions were divided. He wanted to defeat Great Britain, but he also fully supported the authority of the monarchy and did not believe the people should have the right to rebel against a king.

The Burgoyne Plan

While Louis wrestled with the issue of backing the American Revolution, events unfolded in America that helped convince the French, as well as the Spanish and Dutch, that they should aid the colonies. Since Trenton and Princeton the British military leadership had been divided on how to prosecute the war. General William Howe proposed to send a massive army to America to crush the rebellion once and for all. In London the British government rejected the plan and instead adopted a plan advanced by General John Burgoyne. Burgoyne proposed to split the colonies into three theaters of war, thus dividing Washington's army into thirds and diminishing its strength.

Under Burgoyne's plan, separate British armies would sweep through the colonies, converging on the New York city of Albany from the north, south, and west. At first the plan appeared to be leading toward success when Howe's army attacked Philadelphia on its march north, taking the capital on September 26, 1777, and forcing the Continental Congress to flee.

But the plan went awry when a British army under Burgoyne encountered American troops at Saratoga, New York. In the late summer of 1777 Burgoyne's army of ten thousand Redcoats and Hessian mercenaries embarked from their encampment in Canada and headed south. Burgoyne's army soon found itself stretched thin—the supply wagons in the rear were unable to keep up with the soldiers leading the march. As Burgoyne's troops marched south they were continually harassed by American snipers in the woods. The colonists also chopped down trees, burned bridges, flooded paths, and did all they could to slow the British advance. Burgoyne's men had to rebuild forty bridges as they marched south.

There were minor skirmishes along the way—all won by the colonists. Burgoyne sent nine hundred men into Bennington, Vermont, to seize provisions and ammunition from colonists. They were met by a militia of two thousand men, who easily defeated the Redcoats.

The Battle of Saratoga

On September 13 Burgoyne crossed the Hudson River, cutting off his army from its supply line. By early October Burgoyne's army was down to fewer than seven thousand men—and they were marching on half-rations. Burgoyne's troops arrived in Saratoga, New York, on October 7. Weary from the long march, their ranks depleted, hungry from marching on half-rations, the Redcoats suddenly found themselves facing an army of ten thousand colonists under the command of General Horatio Gates.

Pierre Beaumarchais, American Revolution Supporter

Before Louis XVI finally agreed to offer overt military and financial aid to the American Revolution in 1778, many private French citizens supported the cause and worked behind the scenes to provide the colonies with arms and money. One of the most influential of these citizens was playwright Pierre Beaumarchais, author of the plays *The Barber of Seville* and *The Marriage of Figaro*.

Beaumarchais was drawn into the cause more so out of a desire to engage in a grand adventure rather than as a believer in democracy and the right of the American people to govern themselves. In May 1776 he convinced Louis XVI to make secret loans to the Continental Congress. "The enemies of our enemies are more than half our friends," he told officials in the French government. He also arranged for rifles, ammunition, and cannons to be shipped to the colonies.

In the summer of 1776 Beaumarchais wrote a letter to Louis spelling out the advantages of aiding the Americans in which he suggested a British victory would result in France losing its colonies in the West Indies. Moreover, he warned Louis that if Great Britain triumphed, the Americans would long blame France for its failure to come to their aid. Says historian David Schoenbrun, "His arguments were cogent, and would be used by [Benjamin] Franklin . . . to persuade a reluctant young King . . . who did not want to go to war with mighty England."

Quoted in Stacy Schiff, *A Great Improvisation: Franklin, France, and the Birth of America*. New York: Henry Holt, 2005, p. 11.

David Schoenbrun, *Triumph in Paris: The Exploits of Benjamin Franklin*. New York: Harper & Row, 1976, pp. 66–67.

It turned out to be more of a massacre than a battle. Burgoyne's men were completely surrounded by American troops, who fired down on the hapless Redcoats and Hessians as they scattered in open meadows. For an entire day and night the colonists hunted down the enemy soldiers, who simply had no place to run. On October 8 the remnants of Burgoyne's army assembled and attempted to slip out of Saratoga, seeking protection at Fort Ticonderoga on Lake Champlain near the Vermont border. But it was pouring rain. Wagons mired in the mud up to their axles. American snipers were still hiding in the trees, and they easily picked off stragglers. Finally realizing the futility of attempting an escape, Burgoyne elected instead to make camp and dig in.

France Recognizes the United States of America

Gates sent an emissary into the camp, offering surrender terms. Negotiations proceeded through the next week until finally, on October 17, 1777, Burgoyne's men laid down their arms and surrendered. They spent the remainder of the Revolution in a prisoner of war camp in Pennsylvania.

Saratoga was the most substantial victory to date in the Revolution: An entire British army had been forced to surrender. News of the American victory reached Paris, where Franklin and Gravier

American general Horatio Gates accepts the surrender of British general John Burgoyne at the close of the Battle of Saratoga. The victory was strategically significant, but it was also politically important because it secured France's entrance into the war on America's side.

pressed Louis to make a commitment to the American Revolution. On February 6, 1778, the French government signed two treaties with the "United States of America." One treaty recognized America as a sovereign nation, pledging French trade and military assistance. As part of the treaty, France agreed to provide military aid to America until independence was achieved. The other treaty pledged American assistance to France should Great Britain make war on France.

Over the next three years the French provided loans totaling some $2 million—an amount that would equal more than $50 million today. The French also sent troops and generals and convinced the monarchs of Spain and Holland to send troops as well. These nations also sent their navies. Within months 150 warships under the French, Spanish, and Dutch flags were patrolling the Atlantic coast, engaging British warships.

A Free and Independent Nation

Other battles followed Saratoga. Some were won by the British, but most were American victories. The final battle of the war, at Yorktown, Virginia, in October 1781, can be directly attributed to aid the American colonists received from the French. Washington, leading a force of eleven thousand soldiers, and a French general, the Marquis de Lafayette, heading an army of five thousand troops, trapped Cornwallis at Yorktown. With their backs to the York River, the Redcoats hoped for reinforcements delivered by the British navy. But on September 5, 1781, a French fleet defeated the English rescue squadron in the Chesapeake Bay before it could enter the York River. Greatly outnumbered, his provisions running low, Cornwallis had no alternative but to surrender.

With few troops remaining in the colonies and no desire to sacrifice more men to what was now a lost cause, Great Britain agreed to recognize the independence of the colonies. The formal treaty was signed in Paris on September 3, 1783.

When the Continental Congress approved the Declaration of Independence, the colonists lacked the financial resources to wage the war as well as arms, ammunition, and military expertise. For help they turned to France, Britain's longtime enemy. The French loans helped America pay for the war, while the French troops, as well as those from Spain and Holland, proved invaluable, helping establish the United States of America as a free and independent nation.

CHAPTER FIVE

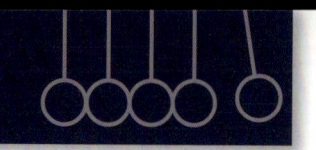

How Did the American Revolution Spark Change Throughout the World?

> **Focus Questions**
> 1. Why do you think Louis XVI helped the Americans establish a democracy yet resisted the movement toward representative government in France?
> 2. What are the common themes that helped spark the French, Russian, and Libyan revolutions?
> 3. Do you think America should provide military aid in places, such as Syria, where oppressed people have struggled to overthrow a dictator? Why or why not?

The impact of the American Revolution was felt beyond the shorelines of the American colonies. The notion that an oppressed people could rise up and, through armed insurrection, topple a monarch was embraced throughout Europe. The first European monarch to feel the wrath of his hungry and abused people was Louis XVI who, ironically, had done so much to aid the cause of democracy in America.

By the mid-1780s the population of France was nearly 25 million. But the vast majority of the country's wealth was controlled by members of an aristocratic class that numbered just twenty-five thousand. French nobles owned sprawling estates and thousands of acres of farmland. Most of the rest of the French population lived as peasants on farms, tilling the fields for their overlords. Those who sought to escape the poverty of rural France flocked to Paris, Marseilles, and other cities. Instead of opportunity they found few jobs, little housing, and squalid conditions. "The misery [in Paris] was acute, aggravated by an influx of provincials attracted by the remote possibility of finding work or assistance in the city when there was none at home," says historian David Garrloch. In his book *The Making of Revolutionary Paris* Garrloch quotes one observer as saying, "Paris is a theater of horrors. The poor besiege us on all sides, they disturb the quiet of the night with cries and sobs, stopping only when they expire." According to Garrloch, another well-to-do citizen of Paris said, "I saw two poor errand boys found dead, completely frozen, in a doorway where they had taken refuge and huddled together to warm themselves."[39]

For much of the eighteenth century serfdom was still a way of life in France—Louis did not free the serfs until 1779. The serfs made up a class of people not much better off than slaves. Serfs lived on the properties of aristocrats to whom they were required to turn over at least half of the crops they tilled. Invariably, their descendants were required to remain in serfdom as well. And yet, once freed by Louis, the former serfs found little opportunity to garner wealth. Says historian Will Durant, "The peasant was left about half the fruit of his toil."[40]

> "I saw two poor errand boys found dead, completely frozen, in a doorway where they had taken refuge and huddled together to warm themselves."[39]
>
> —An anonymous visitor describing Paris in the 1700s.

Liberty, Equality, and Brotherhood

The people of France seethed under the conditions in which they were forced to live. Even aristocrats wondered how much longer the French people would endure their relentless poverty and suggested that for France to survive as a nation, the country must adopt democracy. In 1752 the noble René-Louis de Voyer wrote, "The race of great lords must be destroyed completely. By great lords I understand those who have dignities, property, tithes, offices, and functions and . . . for this reason often [are] worthless."[41]

Louis was virtually powerless to improve the plight of the common people. The Seven Years' War had been as much of a financial hardship on the French government as it had been on the British government. Moreover, making the loans to the American colonies threw the French government further into debt.

Finally, in 1788 Louis agreed to give the French people a voice in their government when he authorized national elections to create an assembly, the Estates-General. On May 5, 1789, the Estates-General convened in Versailles. Soon it became evident the assembly desired more control of the French government than Louis was willing to concede. He responded by locking the members out of their meeting hall. In defiance of Louis, assembly members convened at a nearby tennis court and, in taking what is known as the Tennis Court Oath, swore that they would not dissolve the assembly without writing a new constitution for France. In response, Louis ordered troops to assemble near Paris and Versailles. On July 12 riots erupted as the people of Paris demanded Louis's abdication. Two days later rioters broke into and seized the Bastille, a royal prison that symbolized the despotic regime of the French monarchy. The storming of the Bastille marked the beginning of the end of Louis's regime.

The storming of the Bastille in Paris proved the end of the French monarchy. King Louis XVI had aided America's bid for democracy but was reluctant to cede any power to the revolutionary forces in his own country.

By now the assembly had reconvened. On August 26, 1789, the assembly drafted the Declaration of the Rights of Man and Citizen—a document based on principles espoused in the Declaration of Independence. Louis had no choice but to accept its terms; a year later the French constitution was adopted by the assembly along with the new motto of the French Republic: "*Liberté, Égalité, Fraternité*"—Liberty, Equality, and Brotherhood. These words echoed the principles that inspired the patriots of the American Revolution—principles that had now been adopted by the French.

> "The race of great lords must be destroyed completely."[41]
>
> —French noble René-Louis de Voyer.

Reign of Terror

France's new democracy did not last long. Fervor to depose the king grew within radical quarters of the new government. Demonstrations in the streets were common. Meanwhile, the French faced war from neighboring Austria. Austria's king Francis II hoped to exploit the chaos in France by seizing territory while also reinstating full powers to the French monarchy. (Francis's aunt, Marie-Antoinette, was Louis's wife and thus France's queen.) In April 1792 war broke out between the French and Austrians. Soon other European powers came to the aid of the Austrians.

During the chaos of war a group of insurgents took power in the Estates-General, imprisoned Louis, and on September 21 abolished the French monarchy. On January 21, 1793, Louis was dispatched by the guillotine. Nine months later Marie-Antoinette lost her head as well.

And so began the Reign of Terror, in which an oligarchy known as the Committee of Public Safety suspended the French constitution and oversaw the arrests and executions of thousands of French citizens it believed to be plotting treasonous acts against the government. In this chaos a military officer, Napoleon Bonaparte, rose to prominence and seized control of the French government in 1799. Napoleon ruled as a dictator, restoring order to France and embarking on foreign adventures, enhancing France's position as a military power.

Over the next seven decades the French lived under a series of dictatorial leaders until finally, in 1870, they succeeded in establishing true parliamentary government in what is known as the Third Republic.

Other than the five-year Nazi occupation of France during World War II, the French people have lived since then under democratic governments.

Bloody Sunday

Following the French Revolution more than a dozen European monarchs accepted the establishment of national legislatures in which they shared power with elected citizens. In Russia, however, the czars steadfastly held on to their autocratic power. For decades most of Rus-

Storming the Bastille

During the chaos of the summer of 1789 a mob of some eight thousand Parisians laid siege to the Bastille, a centuries-old prison and fortress. At the time, the Bastille was little used as a prison. In fact, when the rioters broke into the prison they found just seven inmates held in confinement. However, atop the Bastille cannons were aimed at the Parisian neighborhood surrounding the Rue du Faubourg Saint-Antoine, a street that was a hotbed for revolutionary fervor.

At about one o'clock on July 14 eighteen rebels climbed the wall of an adjoining building, leaped onto the roof of the Bastille, and lowered the drawbridges. Hundreds of rioters rushed into the fortress. Inside, they encountered eighty-two French soldiers and thirty-two Swiss guards who fired on the crowd. The rioters fired back. After about two hours of fighting, rebellious members of the French army joined in the siege and bombarded the Bastille with cannon fire. After another two hours under siege, the Bastille's defenders surrendered. The Marquis de Launay, a military officer who led the defense of the Bastille, was taken prisoner by the crowd and murdered.

Louis XVI knew nothing of the siege on the Bastille—he had been on a hunting trip that day. When he returned to his palace he was informed of the siege by an aide, the Duke of Rochefoucauld-Liancourt. "Why," exclaimed Louis, "this is a revolt." "No, Sire," the duke replied, "it is a revolution."

Quoted in Will Durant, *Rousseau and Revolution: The Story of Civilization Part X*. New York: Simon & Schuster, 1967, p. 963.

sia's 130 million people endured relentless poverty, while members of a small aristocracy enjoyed the fruits of the vast country's wealth. Aristocrats and other wealthy Russians owned half of the 8 million acres of agricultural land in Russia. The wealthy also controlled the factories, where pay was low and working conditions often dangerous. Under law, unions were illegal.

During the first decade of the twentieth century, as famine gripped his country, Czar Nicholas II fell under increasing pressure to cede some of his authority to an elected legislature. In 1905 a group of insurgents under the leadership of the Assembly of Russian Workers—an outlawed labor union—staged a street protest in front of the czar's winter palace in St. Petersburg. When nervous soldiers fired into the crowd, killing hundreds, widespread rioting broke out in the Russian capital, leading to a brief—and unsuccessful—revolution against the czar. The events of January 9, 1905, known as Bloody Sunday, have been likened to the Boston Massacre—an act of civil disobedience that helped inspire a revolutionary movement against a monarch.

> "The nature of the [czarist] regime was the single biggest guarantee of its own irreformability. The autocratic ideology of Nicholas II was deeply hostile to the Western constitutional vision ... of reforms."[42]
>
> —Historian Orlando Figes.

After Bloody Sunday Nicholas reluctantly agreed to share power with an elected legislature—the Duma. But he was able to wield considerable authority over the assembly and virtually ignore its legislative actions. Says historian Orlando Figes,

> The nature of the [czarist] regime was the single biggest guarantee of its own irreformability. The autocratic ideology of Nicholas II was deeply hostile to the Western constitutional vision ... of reforms. Perhaps we should ask if any package of political reforms could have resolved the social problems that led to the revolution of 1905. Could the land question—the main concern of the majority of the population—have been resolved without the confiscation of the gentry's land? Would the workers have been satisfied with the moderate proposals of the Duma to improve conditions in the factories and allow limited trade union rights? The answer to these questions must be "no."[42]

The rule of Nicholas finally collapsed in February 1917, in the midst of World War I. At the time, Russia had suffered numerous battlefield losses against Germany, while at home the Russian people endured a lack of food and fuel to heat their homes. When Nicholas refused to open warehouses where grain was stored, insurgents rioted in the streets. When the insurgents were joined by troops sent by Nicholas to put down the rioting, the Duma seized power and forced Nicholas to abdicate. As in the American Revolution, a violent uprising against a monarch had resulted in the establishment of a democracy but—like the French Revolution—the initial attempt to establish a representative government in Russia soon collapsed.

The Duma created a Provisional Government, but it never had the support of the people largely because it vowed to continue waging war against Germany. A radical movement known as the Bolsheviks seized power in October 1917. The Bolshevik leader, Vladimir Lenin, promised to withdraw from the war and delivered this message to the Russian people: "Peace, bread, land."[43]

The Reign of Terror in France claimed the lives of tens of thousands considered disloyal to the ideals of the French Revolution. Louis XVI met his end at a Paris guillotine along with his wife and roughly 2,600 other "enemies" of the new state.

Broken Promises

Advocating the ideology of communism, in which all citizens share equally in the wealth of the state, the Bolsheviks at first promised representative government and issued a document that echoed the words of the Declaration of Independence. Issued in November 1917, the Declaration of the Rights of the People of Russia promised:

> The equality and sovereignty of the peoples of Russia.
>
> The right of the peoples of Russia to free self-determination, even to the point of separation and the formation of an independent state.
>
> The abolition of any and all national and national-religious privileges and disabilities.
>
> The free development of national minorities and ethnographic groups inhabiting the territory of Russia.[44]

These promises were not kept. After a four-year civil war in which the Bolsheviks faced anti-Communist forces loyal to the czar or the former Provisional Government, the Bolsheviks emerged as victorious. Lenin died in 1924 and was succeeded by Joseph Stalin, who turned into one of the world's most powerful and vindictive dictators.

Stalin forged the Union of Soviet Socialist Republics, making it into a totalitarian state that endured for nearly forty years after his death in 1953. Only after the Soviet Union collapsed in 1991 would the Russian people write a new constitution, embrace democracy, and pick their leaders through popular elections.

Arab Spring

In the years since the people of the former Soviet Union forged new democracies, other oppressed peoples in the world rose against tyrants who denied them the principles of democracy, self-determination, and economic opportunity that were first enunciated in the Declaration of Independence more than two centuries ago. In late 2010 a series of protests erupted in several countries in the Middle East and North Africa as people long-oppressed by dictators demanded human rights and the establishment of democratic governments. In Jordan and Oman, monarchs agreed to reforms that provided their citizens with more representation in their governments.

But in Bahrain, King Hamad bin Isa bin Salman Al Khalifa had no interest in turning his regime into a representative government; he used strong-arm tactics to put down the protests and arrest insurgents. In Syria, a civil war erupted against the rule of longtime dictator Bashar al-Assad that by 2015 was still being waged. But in three countries—Tunisia, Egypt, and Libya—dictators were ousted after citizens rose up in defiance during a period known as the Arab Spring.

The regimes in Egypt and Tunisia fell in early 2011 after the militaries in those countries refused to fire on their own citizens. In Libya, though, the military stayed loyal to dictator Muammar Gaddafi, forcing insurgents to wage an armed conflict that took nearly a year to topple the tyrant.

Rise and Fall of Muammar Gaddafi

Throughout much of the twentieth century the North African nation of Libya was one of the poorest countries on earth. Moreover, the country had long been dominated by foreign powers. It was invaded by Italy in the 1920s and, after liberation during World War II, divided among the French and British. Following World War II the newly formed United Nations established Libya as an independent nation. In 1951 the Libyans wrote their first constitution, providing for governance by a monarch and an elected legislature.

During the 1950s the discovery of oil in the Libyan desert helped lift the country out of its relentless poverty, but the rights expressed by the Libyan constitution were short-lived. In 1969 Gaddafi, a young military officer, led a coup against the king and established himself as dictator. During his forty-two-year rule Gaddafi emerged as one of the world's most vindictive and unstable dictators. He abolished the rule of law, tossed his enemies in jail or had them exiled or executed, sponsored international terrorism, and lived an opulent lifestyle even though most of his people subsisted in relentless poverty. Finally, in 2011 an armed insurrection emerged in Libya.

The Libyan Declaration of Independence

In 1951 Libya, a country whose people had been dominated by foreign powers for decades, issued a Declaration of Independence. The Libyan Declaration was incorporated into the country's first constitution, which established the rule of a monarch. But the constitution also created a senate and invested the power to govern in the people of Libya. The Libyan Declaration of Independence includes language that closely resembles the words written by Thomas Jefferson two centuries earlier:

> Libyans shall be equal before the law. They shall enjoy equal civil and political rights, shall have the same opportunities, and be subject to the same public duties and obligations, without distinction of religion, belief, race, language, wealth, kinship or political or social opinions.
>
> Everyone charged with an offence shall be presumed to be innocent until proved guilty according to law in a trial at which he has the guarantees necessary for his defence. The trial shall be public save in exceptional cases prescribed by law.
>
> No one may be arrested, detained, imprisoned or searched except in the cases prescribed by law. No one shall under any circumstances be tortured by anyone or subjected to punishment degrading to him.
>
> Dwelling houses are inviolable; they shall not be entered or searched except in cases and according to the manner prescribed by law.

Says Wafa Bugaighis, an official in the Libyan Education Ministry, "It formally set out rights such as equality before the law, as well as equal civil and political rights, equal opportunities, and an equal responsibility for public duties and obligations."

Quoted in Libyan Constitutional Union, "Libya's Constitution," December 4, 2013. www.lcu-libya.co.uk.

Wafa Bugaighis, "Prospects for Women in New Libya," in Muhamad S. Olimat, ed., *Arab Spring and Arab Women: Challenges and Opportunities*. New York: Routledge, 2014, p. 107.

Libyans celebrate the downfall of the dictatorial government of leader Muammar Gaddafi in 2011. Such struggles for independence—whether from foreign influence or internal despots—continue to demonstrate a global desire for freedom and democracy.

Much like the American colonists of the eighteenth century, the Libyan rebels obtained arms, military advisers, and financial assistance from foreign allies—among them Saudi Arabia, Qatar, and the United Arab Emirates. Leaders of those countries felt threatened by the unstable Libyan dictator. The US, British, and French navies also assisted, sending ships to the Libyan coast and establishing no-fly zones, which assisted the rebels by keeping the Libyan air force on the ground.

As the insurgency grew, Gaddafi's army suffered desertions. On August 21, 2011, armed rebels entered the Libyan capital of Tripoli, where they were welcomed by the city's inhabitants. Gaddafi escaped into the desert, but his convoy was discovered on the morning of October 20 as it attempted to leave the city of Sirte. A French fighter jet attacked the convoy, scattering Gaddafi's bodyguards. Gaddafi stumbled out of his car and hid in a sewer drain. Discovered by rebels, he was dragged through the streets, roughed up, and, finally, executed with a gunshot to the head.

Unique Experiment in Democracy

Since the fall of Gaddafi, democracy has returned to Libya, but the country's government is by no means stable. By 2015 Libya was teetering on the brink of civil war. The country is under siege by a number of rebel groups. Some wish to establish a fundamentalist Islamic regime, while other rebel groups desire to seize the country's oil industry to attain great wealth. During the fighting nearly three hundred thousand Libyans have been forced to flee their homes to escape the violence.

Like the French and Russians before them, the Libyans found their fight for democracy did not end after they unseated tyrants. Following the American Revolution the colonists joined together in a spirit of unity and in 1787 drafted a strong constitution that united the thirteen colonies. The American Revolution culminated in a unique experiment in democracy that other nations have been hard-pressed to duplicate.

SOURCE NOTES

Introduction: Assault on Breed's Hill
1. Quoted in Kenneth Roberts, *Rabble in Arms*. New York: Doubleday, 2012, ebook.
2. John Ferling, "Myths of the American Revolution," *Smithsonian*, January 2010. www.smithsonianmag.com.
3. Benson Bobrick, *Angel in the Whirlwind: The Triumph of the American Revolution*. New York: Simon & Schuster, 1997, p. 142.
4. Quoted in Independence Hall Association, "Temple's Diary," 2014. www.ushistory.org.
5. Quoted in Bobrick, *Angel in the Whirlwind*, p. 143.
6. Quoted in Gordon S. Wood, *The American Revolution: A History*. New York: Modern Library, 2002, p. 54.

Chapter One: A Brief History of the American Revolution
7. Thomas Paine, *Common Sense*, Independence Hall Association, 2014. www.ushistory.org.
8. Wood, *The American Revolution: A History*, pp. 3–4.
9. Quoted in Bobrick, *Angel in the Whirlwind*, p. 29.
10. Quoted in PBS, *Freedom: A History of US*, "The Shot Heard 'Round the World," 2002. www.pbs.org.
11. Quoted in Robert Middlekauff, *The Glorious Course: The American Revolution, 1763–1789*. New York: Oxford University Press, 1982, p. 269.
12. Quoted in Middlekauff, *The Glorious Course*, p. 270.

Chapter Two: How Did the Actions by the King and Parliament Give Rise to the Revolution?
13. Middlekauff, *The Glorious Course*, p. 57.
14. Middlekauff, *The Glorious Course*, p. 148.
15. Quoted in Wood, *The American Revolution: A History*, pp. 34–35.
16. Wood, *The American Revolution: A History*, pp. 37–38.
17. Quoted in Richard R. Beeman, *Our Lives, Our Fortunes & Our Sacred Honor: The Forging of American Independence, 1774–1776*. New York: Basic Books, 2013, p. 331.

Chapter Three: How Did the Battles of Trenton and Princeton Change the Course of the Revolution?

18. Graeme Kent, *On the Run: Deserters Through the Ages*. London: Robson, 2013, ebook.
19. Quoted in Bruce Lancaster, *The American Heritage History of the American Revolution*. New York: Simon & Schuster, 2003, p. 179.
20. John Tebbel, *Turning the World Upside Down: Inside the American Revolution*. New York: Orion, 1993, p. 127.
21. Quoted in Bobrick, *Angel in the Whirlwind*, p. 209.
22. Quoted in Bobrick, *Angel in the Whirlwind*, p. 215.
23. Quoted in Frederick Fooy, "Bloodshed in Brooklyn," *South Brooklyn Post*, November 13, 2011. http://southbrooklynpost.com.
24. Quoted in Bobrick, *Angel in the Whirlwind*, p. 229.
25. Quoted in History.com, "Thomas Paine Publishes *An American Crisis*," 2014. www.ushistory.org.
26. Quoted in Lancaster, *The American Heritage History of the American Revolution*, p. 189.
27. Quoted in Bobrick, *Angel in the Whirlwind*, p. 233.
28. Quoted in Lancaster, *The American Heritage History of the American Revolution*, p. 189.
29. Quoted in Bobrick, *Angel in the Whirlwind*, p. 233.
30. Quoted in Todd Andrlik, ed., *Reporting the Revolutionary War*. Naperville, IL: Sourcebooks, 2012, p. 212.
31. Quoted in Bobrick, *Angel in the Whirlwind*, p. 235.
32. Bruce Chadwick, "Battles of Trenton and Princeton," in Andrlik, ed., *Reporting the Revolutionary War*, p. 210.
33. Quoted in Don N. Hagist, "Top 10 Battles of the Revolutionary War," *Journal of the American Revolution*, September 17, 2013. http://allthingsliberty.com.

Chapter Four: How Did Assistance from France Help the American Cause?

34. Quoted in David Schoenbrun, *Triumph in Paris: The Exploits of Benjamin Franklin*. New York: Harper & Row, 1976, p. 42.
35. Charles Rappleye, *Robert Morris: Financier of the American Revolution*. New York: Simon & Schuster, 2010, p. 108.

36. Quoted in Dan Shippey and Michael Burns, "Not Worth a Continental Dollar," Breed's Hill Institute, 2009. www.breedshill.org.
37. Quoted in Wood, *The American Revolution: A History*, p. 77.
38. Quoted in Schoenbrun, *Triumph in Paris: The Exploits of Benjamin Franklin*, p. 81.

Chapter Five: How Did the American Revolution Spark Change Throughout the World?

39. David Garrloch, *The Making of Revolutionary Paris*. Berkeley, CA: University of California Press, 2004, p. 46.
40. Will Durant, *Rousseau and Revolution: The Story of Civilization Part X*. New York: Simon & Schuster, 1967, p. 929.
41. Quoted in Durant, *Rousseau and Revolution: The Story of Civilization Part X*, p. 930.
42. Orlando Figes, *Revolutionary Russia 1891–1991: A History*. New York: Metropolitan, 2014, p. 50.
43. Quoted in BBC, "The Provisional Government and Its Problems," 2014. www.bbc.co.uk.
44. Quoted in Marxists.org, "Declaration of the Rights of the People of Russia," 2006. www.marxists.org.

FOR FURTHER RESEARCH

Books
Todd Andrlik, ed., *Reporting the Revolutionary War*. Naperville, IL: Sourcebooks, 2012.

Richard R. Beeman, *Our Lives, Our Fortunes & Our Sacred Honor: The Forging of American Independence, 1774–1776*. New York: Basic Books, 2013.

Walter R. Borneman, *American Spring: Lexington, Concord, and the Road to Revolution*. New York: Little, Brown and Co., 2014.

Orlando Figes, *Revolutionary Russia 1891–1991: A History*. New York: Metropolitan, 2014.

Jonathan Israel, *Revolutionary Ideas: An Intellectual History of the French Revolution from the Rights of Man to Robespierre*. Princeton, NJ: Princeton University Press, 2014.

Eric Nelson, *The Royalist Revolution: Monarchy and the American Founding*. Cambridge, MA: Harvard University Press, 2014.

Andrew Jackson O'Shaughnessy, *The Men Who Lost America: British Leadership, the American Revolution, and the Fate of the Empire*. New Haven, CT: Yale University Press, 2013.

Nathaniel Philbrick, *Bunker Hill: A City, a Siege, a Revolution*. New York: Penguin, 2014.

Websites
The American Revolution: Lighting Freedom's Flame (www.nps.gov/revwar). Maintained by the National Park Service, the website provides a timeline of the Revolution as well as essays on the causes of the war, the role of privateers, and biographies of figures in the Revolution, including Thomas Paine and George Washington. Students can also take a virtual tour of battle sites of the Revolution.

The American War of Independence: The Rebels and the Redcoats (www.bbc.co.uk/history/british/empire_seapower/rebels_redcoats_01.shtml#four). The website maintained by the BBC tells the story of the Revolution from the British point of view. Authored by Richard Holmes, a professor at Cranfield University in Bedford, England, the site includes articles on the causes of the war, British military strategy, and the involvement of the French in the conflict.

Breed's Hill Institute (www.breedshill.org). Established to foster education on the American Revolution, Breed's Hill Institute has established a website that includes the texts of many documents from the colonial era, including Thomas Paine's *Common Sense*. Students can also find essays on the taxation policies of the British Parliament, worthlessness of the continental dollars, and the Battle of Trenton.

French and Indian War/Seven Years' War, 1754–63 (https://history.state.gov/milestones/1750-1775/french-indian-war). The website, maintained by the US State Department, provides an overview of the French and Indian War. By following links on the site, students can read about the causes of the war, the 1763 Treaty of Paris, and the attempts by the British Parliament to pay its war debts by taxing the American colonists.

Journal of the American Revolution (http://allthingsliberty.com). This online magazine includes interviews with historians on such topics as the Battle of Saratoga and Benjamin Franklin's diplomatic mission to France. Students can also find essays by historians on how the American and British newspapers of the era covered the war.

Liberty! The American Revolution (www.pbs.org/ktca/liberty). The companion website to the 2004 PBS series includes descriptions of many important events in the Revolution, including the Boston Tea Party, signing of the Declaration of Independence, and Battle of Yorktown. Students can read essays on daily life in the colonies and events during the era that occurred elsewhere in the world.

Washington Crossing Historic Park (www.washingtoncrossingpark.org). Maintained by the Friends of Washington Crossing Park, the site provides an overview of the Pennsylvania state park established on the site of George Washington's 1776 crossing of the Delaware River. Visitors can read about historically significant places in the park and watch videos of the annual Christmas day reenactment of the crossing.

INDEX

Note: Boldface page numbers indicate illustrations.

Adams, Abigail, 40–41
Adams, John, 30, 34
Allegheny Mountains, 25–27
American Crisis, An (Paine), 43
Arab Spring, 67–71, **70**
Assad, Bashar al-, 68
Austria, 63

Bahrain, 68
Barrington, William, 29
Bastille, storming of, 62, **62**, 64
Beaumarchais, Pierre, 57
Bloody Sunday, 64–66
Bobrick, Benson, 10
Bolsheviks, 66–67
Boston, Massachusetts, 8–9, **9**, 11, 18
Boston Massacre (1770), 16, 29, **29**, 30
Boston Tea Party (1773), 17, 30–31, **31**
Breed's Hill, Battle of, 8–11, **9**
British East India Company, 17
Brooklyn, Battle of, 21, 38–40, **39**, 41
Buchanan, John, 19
Bugaighis, Wafa, 69
Bunker Hill, Battle of, 8–11, **9**
Burgoyne, John
    Battle of Saratoga, 56–58, **58**
    on colonial militiamen, 8
    plan to defeat Americans, 56
    surrender at Saratoga, 21

Canada, 20, 36
causes of the American Revolution
    Quartering Act, 27
    taxes
        colonial responses to, 15, **16**, 28–31, **29**, **31**
        items taxed, 15, 16, 27–28
        method of imposing, 12
        reason for, 25
Chadwick, Bruce, 47
Charlestown peninsula, Massachusetts, 8–11, **9**
Coercive Acts (1774), 17, 31
colonies
    debt from militias for French and Indian War, 15
    life in, 14
    map, **14**
    responses to taxes, 15, **16**, 28–31, **29**, **31**
    See also Continental Congresses
Committee of Public Safety, 63
Common Sense (Paine), 12–13
communism, 66–67
Concord, Battle of, 18–20
Continental Army
    in Canada, 20, 36
    conditions in, 51
    desertions, 36–37, 39, 40
    enlistments, 40, 41, 47
    established, 20
    Washington appointed commander of, 20
    See also specific battles
Continental Congresses
    attack on Philadelphia and, 56
    Continental Army and, 20, 40
    currency printed by, 50–51
    debate over independence, 32–34
    Declaration of Independence
        message to France in, 52
        purpose of Revolution in, 12
        writing and adoption of, 21, 34
    Franklin mission to France, 21, 48
    Olive Branch Petition, 32
    reason for convening, 31–32
    reason for First, 17
    US Navy and, 48
Continental Journal (newspaper), 44–45
continentals, 50–51
Cornwallis, Lord Charles, 22, 41, 45–46, 59
Cowpens, Battle of, 19, 22

Declaration of Independence
    message to France in, 52
    purpose of Revolution in, 12
    writing and adoption of, 21, 34
Declaration of the Rights of Man and Citizen, 63
Declaration of the Rights of the People of Russia, 67
Declaratory Act (1766), 15
Dickinson, John, 32
Dubourg, Barbeu, 49–50
Duma, 65, 66
Durant, Will, 61

economy, 50–51
effects of the American Revolution
    Arab Spring, 67–71, **70**
    creation of new type of government, 12
    French Revolution, **62**, 62–63, 64, **66**
    on Great Britain, 55
    Russian Revolution and communism, 65–67
    shattering of traditional patterns of life, 13
Egypt, 68
Estates-General, 62–63

Ferling, John, 8
Figes, Orlando, 65
Forrest, Thomas, 44
France
    aid to colonies, 59
        guns, 49–50
        loans, 51
        from private citizens, 22, 57
    conditions in, 60–61

Declaration of Independence, 52
Franklin mission to, 21
    Battle of Saratoga and, 58–59
    Battles of Trenton and Princeton and, 54
    departure, 48
    French military advisors to America, 54
    opening of French ports to American privateers, 54
    recognition of American independence, 54–55
    treaties signed, 58–59
Libyan revolution and, 70
military aid from, 22
relations with Great Britain
    history of, 52, **53**
    Seven Years' War, 13–15, 24–25, **26,** 52
revolution in, **62,** 62–63, 64, **66**
Francis II (king of Austria), 63
Franklin, Benjamin, **49**
as colonial diplomat in London, 33
Illinois Company and, 27
mission to France, 21
    Battle of Saratoga and, 58–59
    Battles of Trenton and Princeton and, 54
    departure, 48
    French military advisors to America, 54
    opening of French ports to American privateers, 54
    recognition of American independence, 54–55
    treaties signed, 58
French and Indian War (1754–1763), 13–15, 24–25, **26,** 52
fur trade, 14, 26–27

Gaddafi, Muammar, 68, 70
Garrloch, David, 61
Gaspee (British warship), 29
Gates, Horatio, 56–58, **58**
George III (king of Great Britain)
mercenaries hired by, 33
opinion of colonial militiamen, 8
Proclamation of 1763, 25–26
See also Great Britain
Gravier, Charles, 15, 58–59
Great Britain
colonial settlements west of Allegheny Mountains, 25–27
effects of American victory on, 55
Libyan revolution and, 70
navy, 34, 37–38
Redcoats, 10–11, 17–20, 46, 47
relations with France
    history of, 52, **53**
    Seven Years' War, 13–15, 24–25, **26,** 52
soldiers sent to colonies, 16
taxes imposed by
    British reactions to colonial responses, 28–29, 31, 32
    colonial responses to, 15, **16,** 28–31, **29, 31**
    items taxed, 15, 16, 27–28

method used, 12
reason for, 25
use of Hessian mercenaries, 33, 37
See also specific battles

Hamad bin Isa bin Salman Al Khalifa (king of Bahrain), 68
Hancock, John, 21, 34
Hessian mercenaries
    Battle of Brooklyn, 38, 39
    Battle of Trenton, 41–43, **42,** 44–45, **45**
    hired, 33
    in New York, 37–38
Hewes, Joseph, 32
Holland, 55, 59
Howe, William, 10–11, 41, 55–56
Hundred Years' War (1337–1453), 52, **53**
Hutchinson, Thomas, 30

Illinois Company, 27
Indians and Proclamation of 1763, 25–27
Intolerable Acts (1774), 17, 31

Jefferson, Thomas, and Declaration of Independence, 12, 21, 34, 52
Joan of Arc, 52, **53**
Jordan, 68

Kent, Graeme, 36
Kings Mountain, Battle of, 22

Lafayette, Marquis de, 22, 59
Launay, Marquis de, 64
Lee, Henry, 23
Lenin, Vladimir, 66, 67
Lexington, Battle of, 17–18, 20, **20**
Libya, 68–71, **70**
Libyan Declaration of Independence, 69
London Chronicle (newspaper), 46
Long Island, Battle of, 21, 38–40, **39,** 41
Louis XVI (king of France), 54–55, 57, 61–63
See also France
loyalists, 31–32

Making of Revolutionary Paris, The (Garrloch), 61
Marie-Antoinette (queen of France), 63
Martin, Joseph Plumb, 51
Massachusetts, 15, 17, 28–29
See also specific battles; specific cities
McCurtin, Daniel, 37
McIntosh, Ebenezer, 28
Middlekauff, Robert, 23, 25, 27, 40
militiamen
    Battle of Breed's Hill, 8–11, **9**
    Battles of Lexington and Concord, 17–20, **20**
    British opinion of, 8
    desertions, 36–37, 39, 40
    French and Indian War, 13–15
    tactics of, 11, 18–19
Minden, Battle of, **26**

Minutemen. *See* militiamen
Molly (merchant ship), 48
Morgan, Daniel, 19

Napoleon Bonaparte, 63
New York, 37–38
Nicholas II (czar of Russia), 65–66
North, Lord Frederick, 8, 31

Olive Branch Petition (1775), 32
Oman, 68

Paine, Thomas, 12–13, 43
Paris, Treaty of (1763), 25, 26, 52
Paris, Treaty of (1783), 23, 59
Parker, John, 17, 18
Penn, William, 32
Pennsylvania, 32
Philadelphia, Pennsylvania, 33, 56
    See also Continental Congresses
Pitcairn, John, 18
Prescott, William, 9, 10
Princeton, Battle of, 40, 46–47
    in British press, 46
Proclamation of 1763, 25–27
Prohibitory Act (1776), 32
Prussia, 24–25, **26**

Quartering Act (1765), 27
Quebec, Battle of, 20, 36
Quincy, Josiah, 30

Rall, Johann, 43, 44, **45**
Rappleye, Charles, 50
Redcoats, 10–11, 18–20, 46–47
    See also specific battles
Reign of Terror, 63, **66**
Reprisal (American warship), 48
Rochefoucauld-Liancourt, Duke of, 64
Roebuck (British warship), 33
Russia, 64–67

Saratoga, Battle of, 21, 56–58, **58**
Scammel, Alexander, 23
Schoenbrun, David, 57
serfdom, 61
Serle, Ambrose, 38
Seven Years' War (1756–1763)
    cost of, 15, 25
    defeat of France, 52
    in Europe, 24–25
    in North America, 13–15, **26**
Smith, Francis, 18
Soviet Union, 67
Spain, 54, 55, 59
Stalin, Joseph, 67
Stamp Act (1765), 15, 27, 28
Stamp Act Congress (1765), 15, 28
Sugar Act (1764), 15, 27–28

Syria, 68

Tarleton, Banastre, 19
taxes
    Continental Congress and, 50
    imposed by Great Britain
        British reactions to colonial responses, 28–29, 31, 32
        colonial responses to, 15, **16**, 28–31, **29**, **31**
        items taxed, 15, 16, 27–28
        method used to, 12
        reason for, 25
tea, 16–17
Tebbel, John, 37–38, 40
ten-dollar bonuses, 47
Tennis Court Oath, 62
Thacher, James, 47
Thanksgiving, in Continental Army, 51
Townshend, Charles, 15–16
Townshend Acts (1767), 15–17, 27, 28
Treaty of Paris (1763), 25, 26, 52
Treaty of Paris (1783), 23, 59
Trenton, Battle of, 21
    Cornwallis and, 45–46
    described, 44–45, **45**
    importance of, 47, 54
    preparation of Continental Army, 40, 43
    troop deployments, 41–43, **42**
    weather, 43–44
Tunisia, 68

Union of Soviet Socialist Republics, 67
US Constitution, 30
US Navy, 48

Valley Forge, Pennsylvania, 21, 23
von Steubin, Friedrich Wilhelm, 23
Voyer, René-Louis de, 61

warfare
    tactics of militiamen, 11, 18–19
    tactics of regular armies, 10
Washington, George
    appointed commander of Continental Army, 20
    Battle of Brooklyn (Long Island) and, 38–39, 41
    Battle of Trenton and, 21
    Battle of Yorktown and, 22, 59
    desertions from Continental Army and, 37, 39, 40
    on need for funds, 51
    number of troops commanded by, 40, 41
    at Valley Forge, 21, 23
Washington, William, 19
Wayne, Anthony, 23
westward expansion and Proclamation of 1763, 25–27
Wood, Gordon, 13, 31
World War I, 66

Yorktown, Battle of, 22, 59

PICTURE CREDITS

Cover: Thinkstock Images

Maury Aaseng: 42

© adoc-photos/Corbis: 66

© Bettmann/Corbis: 29, 31

© Corbis: 39

© Akram Elsadawie/Demotix/Corbis: 70

© Leemage/Corbis: 53

Thinkstock Images: 6, 7, 62

Steve Zmina: 14

View of Boston and the Battle of Bunker Hill, 17 June 1775 (colour litho), American School, (18th century)/Private Collection/Peter Newark American Pictures/Bridgeman Images: 9

Boston citizens tar and feather a tax collector (colour litho), American School/Private Collection/Peter Newark Pictures/Bridgeman Images: 16

The Fight on Lexington Common, April 19, 1775, from 'The Story of the Revolution' by Woodrow Wilson (1856–1924), published in Scribner's Magazine, January 3, 1898 (oil on canvas), Pyle, Howard (1853–1911)/Delaware Art Museum, Wilmington, USA/Howard Pyle Collection/Bridgeman Images: 20

The Battle of Minden, c.1760s (coloured etching), English School, (18th century)/Brown University Library, Providence, Rhode Island, USA/Bridgeman Images: 26

Surrender of Colonel Rall at the Battle of Trenton, December 26th, 1776, 1858 (oil on cardboard), Chappel, Alonzo (1828–87)/© Chicago History Museum, USA/Bridgeman Images: 45

Benjamin Franklin, 1766 (colour litho), Martin, David (1736/7–98) (after)/Private Collection/Peter Newark American Pictures/Bridgeman Images: 49

The Surrender of General John Burgoyne at the Battle of Saratoga, 7th October 1777, engraved by Godefroy (coloured engraving), Fauvel, (18th century)/Bibliotheque Nationale, Paris, France/Archives Charmet/Bridgeman Images: 58